Son of the Mountain King

O.R. Sykora

Cover Art by *Nicola Martinez*
Harbourlight Books, a division of Pelican Ventures, LLC
www.pelicanbookgroup.com PO Box 1738 *Aztec, NM * 87410
Harbourlight Books sail and mast logo is a trademark of Pelican Ventures, LLC

Publishing History
First Harbourlight Edition, 2025
Electronic Edition ISBN 978-1-5223-0510-1
Published in the United States of America

PROLOGUE

That night, the familiar squeak of wood rent the air as Mesda shoved closed the old oak door. A shaft of light poured through a gap at the bottom. As this part of the castle was rarely visited after dark, she did not worry about being seen.

This story had begun long before.

That night, an old woman spread a large piece of parchment on the rough table, unaware at that time of how many lives would be affected by what she was to record. A sense of urgency bade Mesda hurry the work that must be finished in the coming hours. Dragging the other two pieces of furniture in what she liked to call her "cell," the woman arranged the tools of her trade on a plain cot and turned the three-legged stool until its worn seat faced the table. Time was short. She grumbled as the parchment persisted in rolling like a potato bug. Stones which had chipped from the crumbling walls finally solved the problem. Mesda then placed her two most important objects alongside the parchment: a stained, worn pot of black ink and a graceful quill. With one final critical look at the tip, she sighed and closed her eyes.

Words came to the woman as they always did. Quietly, insistently. Her hand flew across the page.

Strong, elegant, like a heron soaring over the Great River. Words poured out until precise black marks flooded the parchment. Her long braid brushed her back with furious rhythm. Hours slipped by, driven by the urgency within to complete the task given by the Master.

The moon had risen high to send light through the tiny upper window before the woman finally paused. Only then did she lower her quill and allow her forehead to drop to the table as she listened.

It was complete.

Mesda stretched her neck and shoulders slowly. Her hands were numb, but she knew pain would come soon, sharp and strong. Meanwhile, the moon gazed through the window, an ancient friend who surely would not tire of an old woman's mumblings. "I am getting old." She winced. Needlelike sensations were beginning at her fingertips. "I do not know why the Master thinks me still worthy of the work." The cot groaned in harmony with her bones as she crawled onto it and lay with a grunt. Surely, her sister would tolerate waiting for a few minutes more.

Her sister.

Mesda stretched, watching the moon. Perhaps her sister was right to pursue a warrior's life instead of a scholar's path. She'd had her excitement, and now she gracefully doled out advice and justice like so many nuggets while the scholar-scribe had continued to work her neck into a spasm. Still… There was honor in all work assigned by the Master, warrior and scribe alike.

Mesda smiled, grateful for her own part, awash with a moment of youth until a twinge in her shoulder brought her back. It was time to rise. By now, her sister would be impatiently waiting to receive the scroll and deliver it yet farther to the governors. Enchanting people, the governors—a baby was soon to be born to the couple in their advanced age. The baby would be a girl, the woman knew, and she was to be betrothed to the Master's son. But Mesda would not be here for the birth. The morrow would bring a welcome journey up the mountain, back to the home she deeply missed during the weeks in this castle cell she had temporarily claimed while waiting to write the Master's words. Now, her mission was complete.

What did the Master mean by saying he had one more task for her to do? Was she to return to Castle Marah some day? In the silence, no answer came, so, as was her custom, she sat again to read the words that had barely dried on the parchment.

Finally, the parchment was ready. A cord, a few beads of hot wax from the candle, a press from the Mountain King's seal, and she was done.

Grumwold was waiting.

CHAPTER 1

Nineteen Years Later

Judah:

I often longed to be a bird. If I had been a bird that day, I would have perched on the great oak growing into the base of the southern guard tower to watch as a procession wound its way down the narrow street to the tiny chapel in the village wall, a slow and silent parade broken by a single pan flute's dirge. Gray skies and irregular cobblestones reflected the somber faces of those who processed. An open casket, barely shielded by darkly transparent cloth, revealed the pale, serene face of the dead. Here an ancient woman rested, with long, pure white hair arranged under a band of silver. The mourning women behind the casket bearers appeared solemnly satisfied that they had been able to give their respects to this great woman.

But I was not a bird, and so instead of hiding in rustling oak leaves, I strode between the casket and the mourning women. My moss-shaded dress covered a heart beating with pain of loss. The swishing veil of mourning felt strange, a midnight waterfall cascading over my gold circlet.

A steadying hand reached out as I faltered on a

loose stone, and I nodded thanks. Dark mountains of dizzying heights loomed behind Castle Marah, visceral and constant. Despite the crowds, I had never felt so alone. I had not quite reached twenty years of age, although already almost three of those years had been marked by my solo rule as governor of the Mountain King's land. Until now, Grumwold had worked by my side. Now, she lay ahead of me at rest, reunited in death with Lord Leo and Lady Elanna, my parents. A single crow called from the wall. I frowned. *A bad omen of things to come?*

My tears had dried some days before—I had known for a long time that this day would arrive, just as fall and winter inevitably follow spring and summer. The autumn season of Grumwold's life had been the days in which she had come to mean so much to me. What had life been like in the days before age—that merciless warden—had slowed and then slain the woman now being carried to her final place of rest?

Grumwold. Head Justice of Marah and its country. I shook off the shudder sparked by the crow—surely only good would come on the day this great woman was lain to rest. Her name had struck fear in the hearts of some, honor and love in the hearts of others, but all, if asked, would have admitted that the name commanded respect. Grumwold, young warrior, head justice, councilor to the governors, beloved tutor and mentor and friend to me. Tales abounded of her reckless—albeit honorable and virtuous—youth. The person I had come to know so well was white-headed, frail in body, sharp in wit, and prone to knitting at any given moment. The same woman responsible for developing the kingdom's impressive justice system was also the recipient of a seemingly never-ending supply of wool. No impoverished person in the country lived without the comfort of a warm, woolen hat brought into being by the incessant needles of Grumwold.

Since the shepherds and flocks had been absent from the kingdom for so many years, Grumwold had frequently been asked about her mysterious supply. Pursed lips and a mischievous wink were the invariable responses to such queries.

I had tried to learn from her, things I knew I would use when my time came to be governor of the land. Grumwold was a second mother to me—not sentimental or prone to false praise, but nonetheless warm, a counselor and guide and friend. She disliked reminiscing, and I never did get much out of her when I begged for stories of her youth. "The past has already been lived," the older woman would calmly reply to my pestering. "Let us focus on today."

One day when I was still a very small girl, however, Grumwold had spoken of wandering with the shepherds before the Destruction. I had noted the unique yarn that Grumwold always used. Common yarn in Marah was spun of goats' hair or coarse horse hair, whereas Grumwold knit with yarn of soft wool. When I asked Grumwold about it, in the way that all children do, Grumwold smiled and told of when she, as a young girl, spent time with the nearby shepherds and their flocks. The shepherds had been very kind to her, taught her the ways of beasts and man and how to live well in the great wild with nothing but a few tools and a creative mind. Even as a little girl, I noticed the change that came over the old woman as she spoke of those days. Grumwold seemed young again, golden and beautiful, with eyes that glowed and sparkled.

"Is that where you get your yarn from then, Lady Grumwold?" I had asked her.

"Yes, child. My yarn and everything else." That was all Grumwold would say.

The second time I remember Grumwold telling stories about her younger days was years later during the night watch after my parents died. Both my mother and father faded away on the same day. I believe the bond uniting them had been so strong that their hearts remained tied in death as they had been in life. That night I prepared to stay up as was the custom, watching until the dawn broke. Stars hung like jewels in the velvet sky. A quiet step told me Grumwold had come. No words, but I understood she would stay and watch with me. Throughout that long night, lit by torches and stars, Grumwold told me stories of being a young warrior before the Destruction, and her role in the reconstruction. When I pressed for details of the rebellion, she reluctantly shared how she had not supported the movement and gathering of troops. "I feared your dear parents had been sadly deceived, more so than anyone realized..." At this, she'd stopped, and her voice trailed off as she walked away. When she returned, she pressed into my hand a tiny golden key on a delicate chain. She said that the key should be kept safe, hidden under my garments.

"What does the key unlock, dear Grumwold?" I had whispered.

"There is a compartment your parents built in the wall behind the painting of their old home, Amia. Inside the compartment, you will find a narrow box made of gold and jewels that was given to protect your betrothal right to the son of the Mountain King. Keep this secret, Judah, until the time is right."

"But how will I know when the time is right?"

A tear formed in Grumwold's eye. "You will know, dear child."

I will never forget that tear.

I clasped the chain around my neck and hid the key under my garments while Grumwold turned toward the valley. A warm breeze caused the torches to flicker and loosened a few strands of her white hair.

The funeral procession for that woman filed into the chapel courtyard. *How much my dear friend had helped me through the days following my parents' deaths...* I pressed the tiny key that still rested over my heart. How does one pay respects and bid farewell to such a friend? How does the world make up for the loss of wisdom and understanding that passes away with such as this woman?

She would tell me, "The wisdom never dies—it lives in the hearts of the wise."

I smiled and straightened. *May I be such a one—may your legacy live on in me and mine, dear Grumwold.*

After the ceremony, I walked slowly up the cobbled street toward the castle, my companions and attendants following closely behind. The wind picked up, and the black veils whirled like dancers moving to a soft requiem. As my small group passed, people nodded, murmuring words of kindness or consolation. Anna and Hilda, my attendants, answered the people's words with quiet thanks. "She was the last one, you know," I suddenly mused aloud.

"The last one, my lady?" Anna struggled with her veil. "This blasted wind," she muttered under her breath.

Hilda snorted and meaningfully tapped the many hairpins that firmly held her own veil in place. Dear Hilda, a practical and composed balance to Anna's turbulence.

I hesitated before turning to my attendants. "The last of the servants and councilors and friends who came from Amia. Grumwold was the last one alive."

Chapter 2

I was not accustomed to spying on my attendants, and that certainly was not my intention now. But I heard voices. The door was already open, and a curtain mostly hid me from their view. I paused and watched. Velvety folds of deep green poured through Hilda's fingers, catching the light like moss in a mountain brook. Hilda smiled, cradling the dress she was mending. Her fingers searched the soft fabric, drawing it taut, feeling irregularities, any pulls or rips or—heaven forbid—holes. She had always held a soft spot for gorgeous fabric. And right now, I envied her peaceful retreat from the strangely subdued days following the funeral. The usual castle bustle maintained a semblance of normalcy, but a distinct change affected the atmosphere. The entire kingdom had relied on Grumwold's wisdom after the death of my parents, not the least because she was the only one left from the days of Amia. And one of the last to have known the world before the Destruction.

An exasperated sigh escaped from Hilda. I cringed—she must have found the tear in the velvet. Forget contemplating the hole in the fabric of our small kingdom. Hilda frowned over having to fix the very real hole that was staring out from the dress in her hands. "How does Lady Judah manage to damage even her fine ceremonial clothes?" she moaned to her companion, Anna, her friend as well as co-attendant, who sat across the room. "It's not like she wore it out riding…or has she?"

Anna laughed, all too aware, I knew, of my habits. I was just about to enter the room when Anna's words caught my attention.

"I'll admit, I've worried for years about how this death would affect Judah," Anna declared. Hilda's mouth was filled with pins, and she merely grunted in reply.

"I even wondered if, well, if Judah might miss Lady Grumwold more than her parents? Not that—" Anna must have noticed the wordless disapproval I was certain lay written all over Hilda's face. "Not that she didn't, of course, *love* her parents dearly, I'm sure. I only wondered whether she felt quite as close to them." Anna paused to shake out the folds of the gown she was repairing.

"Anna, really."

"Don't you raise that eyebrow. Grumwold was usually an old dear, but admit that even you found Lord Leo and Lady Elanna a trifle…*stiff*. Traditional."

"Easy enough to speak of the dead," Hilda returned drily, plucking pins from her mouth before giving the fabric a critical eye.

"Oh pooh, you know what I mean." A fly chose to dive into Anna's face.

Hilda dodged a wild swing that narrowly missed her head and nearly rolled on the floor as Anna lost her balance and tumbled backward over a nearby trunk.

I slapped a hand over my mouth, my shoulders shaking, as Hilda shrieked in laughter at Anna's feet pointing skyward.

Anna finally managed to scramble up, glaring balefully at her.

"Someone else I know is going to feel a *trifle stiff* tomorrow, I think," Hilda choked back her laughter.

"Aren't we just the circus." Anna scowled and stomped off to pout by the pile of gowns.

"I don't know that *we* are, but I believe someone may have received what she deserved."

"Why? I'm not afraid to share my mind. I'm perfectly comfortable saying what I think about the previous governors, and further that Grumwold herself often displayed touches of tyranny that I'm afraid have started to rub off on—"

"Rub off on whom, might I ask?" I stepped forward and leaned against the doorway doing my best to look, I'm afraid, mildly annoyed.

"Hilda," Anna finished lamely, patting her disheveled hair and sitting, the impression of a deflated wild woman.

I snorted.

"Oh, Hilda. But, of course. Hilda can be such a tyrant at times, can't she?"

Hilda serenely pulled the final pins from her mouth. "Guilty as charged, I'm sure."

"Well, whether guilty or not, I have news that might interest you both. An envoy is on its way to the castle as we speak." I yawned.

Anna and Hilda jumped up.

"I understand," I continued with a smile, "they come from the Mountain King." At these words, Anna squealed.

Hilda laid aside her mending and threw open the wardrobe doors. All of us loved the drama of preparing for a reception.

The welcoming trumpets resounded from the village walls and watchtowers. Where all had been quiet only minutes before, excitement buzzed, and doors and shutters banged open. I could see the familiar sight in my mind's eye: villagers crowding the streets to cheer the fine procession marching through the gate, up the main street, and into the castle. Elegant mantles displaying the Mountain King's colors, pure white and sky blue, bedecking an impressive company. Children skipping along behind the procession, making it to the castle doors and dashing giggling back to their parents at the very last moment when the great door opened grandly.

It always amused me that most of the castle servants would vie for spots around the windows to catch a glimpse of the visitors. For though this was not the first time an envoy had been sent here from the palace of the Mountain King, as all people who live in castles—or villages, for that matter—know, any occurrence is a welcome break from routine.

As my attendants arranged the ceremonial robes and gave me a final look-over, the ancient hinges of the castle doors groaned, and voices floated upward. Below, I knew elegant greetings would be exchanged before the head steward would skillfully steer the company into the great hall. Only a few minutes remained.

We three rushed along the passageway.

The company was greeted again by trumpets.

There was the door. A pause, a signal, more trumpets shouted, and doors opened.

I stepped forward.

All those in the room arose.

"Lady Judah, ruling governor over the land under the Mountain King," a herald announced.

I crossed the hall to the raised platform where four throne-like chairs still sat: two for my parents, one for me, and one for Advisor-in-Chief Grumwold. I couldn't bear moving the other three just yet, so I left them alone.

I proceeded directly to the chief messenger and dropped a deep curtsy.

He bowed his head and kissed my hand respectfully as I stood. "Your ladyship is well, I trust?"

"Lord Gregory. Thank you, yes. And your lordship?"

He smiled as we reached the platform and sat down. "Very well. The journey was refreshing. We made remarkably good time." I raised an eyebrow to Anna and Hilda, and they stopped arranging my robes and scooted off the dais.

"I hope all is well in the palace of the Mountain King."

Lord Gregory accepted the proffered wine and sipped, his face kind and gracious. I had always liked his warm, open ways. "All are most definitely well. His Majesty sends greetings to you, his governor and betrothed of his son. He also greets all who are yours." He leaned closer and lowered his voice. "We were very sorry to hear of your loss. Lady Grumwold was beloved by all who knew her—a truly great lady." He studied my face and chuckled. "You are surprised, I think."

Grumwold—beloved and known by those in the palace of the Mountain King himself. I blushed. Apparently, he had read my expression and understood my thoughts. Truly the secrets of Grumwold were beyond measure. "I have always known she was a great lady," I affirmed.

"But perhaps you were unaware of her connections?"

I smiled. "The greatest people are also the ones who conceal their height from the sight of others." I leaned forward. "Did you know her personally?"

"I wish I had had the privilege of closer acquaintance, but I was limited to association from a distance. I admired her exceedingly." He glanced toward the extra chairs on the dais. "Her presence here is missed, I think."

I lowered my eyes.

Lord Gregory—rather tactfully—changed topics and raised his voice. "But I neglect my duties. Special greetings are sent to her ladyship from the son of the Mountain King. He gives not only his best regards but also hopes that the Lady Judah will accept these humble gifts from his hand."

This was always my favorite part.

At a signal, a few young men stepped forward bearing beautifully ornamented boxes. The wood was intricately carved with mountain settings and animals, with graceful accents of gold and precious stones. The first young man came forward to present his box, and as he raised the lid, I gasped at the contents. A glow emanated from a folded fabric. Putting the box down, the young man carefully lifted the gift. It was a robe of the most delicate fabric, with designs reflecting the beautiful scenes of the box. The threads were gold, catching and flashing light around the room. I had never seen anything so lovely, so perfect, and it was a struggle to maintain my composure in the face of this regal gift. I signaled an attendant to collect the present.

The second young man brought his box, which, when opened, contained a letter fastened with the royal seal. Having received gifts from previous envoys on behalf of the Mountain King's son, I was not surprised by this gift. I once again nodded my gratitude.

To my surprise, a third young man advanced.

Alongside him stood a rather ugly old woman clad in plain, homespun clothes. A long, white braid hung down her back. The woman bore deep wrinkles and a squint that reminded me of the dried apple faces children carve in the wintertime. *What in the world? Why is she here?*

Lord Gregory was smiling. "Lady Judah, I present the final gift from the son of the Mountain King. I present Mesda."

CHAPTER 3

I was always told a leader must never show her reaction to an awkward situation, but my eyebrow flickered. I couldn't help it. The son of the Mountain King had sent an old woman? What did this mean? I coughed discreetly and inhaled. *Is this…a joke?* "Welcome, Mesda." I glanced at the chief messenger, desperately seeking a clue.

My servants whispered behind me.

"Mesda will remain here in the castle at your service, my lady."

Mesda's eyes twinkled at me as she lowered her head. "My lady."

"Ah… Well… Delightful—many thanks." Where were Anna and Hilda? They had been here a moment ago. What was I expected to do? She was dressed as a servant. *Perhaps the cook can use her?* I caught the eye of a courtier who met my gaze and nodded for him to remove the old woman. I smiled anew at Lord Gregory. "Please convey to the son of the Mountain King my humble gratitude for his generosity and kindness, these most wonderful and…unusual gifts."

"And a letter for His Majesty?"

"Yes—it will be delivered to your care on the morrow." I stood up. "And now, if his lordship and esteemed company would grace us with the favor of remaining as our guests for the night, I believe the time for dinner has come."

~*~

I have always loved the dining hall. Most nights I ate alone in the privacy of a small library or in my own chambers. However, I relished the rare opportunities for banqueting with guests, and tonight, the dining hall was laid out with marvelous dishes, a feast for a king. Servants bustled like so many honeybees, refilling steaming platters, pouring wine, and mopping up the occasional spill. The head cook had outdone herself, the intertwining aromas of rich sauces, fluffy pastries, exotic moist meats, steaming breads, crisp vegetables, and ripe fruit culminating in sensory, culinary intoxication. A few musicians played lively tunes in the corner, and here and there a child could be seen sneaking a choice morsel before flying down the hall with triumphant squeals. A fire blazed on one side of the room. An army of torches and candles made the rich tapestries and paintings lining the walls glow. It was entrancing.

From a discreet corner, the elderly head steward—who as far as I could tell, never condescended to looking happy, on principle—allowed himself a rare indulgence of a barely relaxed mouth. Not quite a smile—heavens, no—but mildly appreciative, like a frog evaluating a particularly pleasant bit of marsh. He caught my eye, and I smiled appreciation.

If the head steward had observed more closely, he may have noticed my fidgetiness. And if he had guessed my movements expressed anxiety, he would have been correct. I *was* nervous. I traced the glass sparkling in my hand and wrinkled my nose to rally my spirits. *Now is as good a time as any.* Taking a slow, deep breath, I turned to the chief messenger next to me. "Lord Gregory."

"My lady." He put down his glass and turned, smiling kindly.

"I have a question, my heart has long desired to know the answer," I continued, fiddling with the linen under the table. *Calm down.*

"I hope to assist you in any way."

"May his lordship not think me bold, but—why has the son of the Mountain King never come himself to see me?" *There.*

"That, I could not say, my lady," the man replied, brushing flakes of pastry from his beard, "for I have not been told, and one cannot guess the ways of the Mountain King, nor of his son."

My face fell.

"I believe, though," he added, "that the time will not be long before he himself comes. And," he said with a significant smile, "may glad tidings of a wedding be given shortly thereafter." He raised his glass to me.

I blushed. "Thank you. As deeply appreciative as I am for the many exquisite gifts, a lady finds it strange when the wooer himself does not come to woo."

"Touché." He laughed.

"Perhaps my lord would be kind enough to at least describe the man who sends me letters and gifts?" Now was not the moment for demureness. I wanted information. "Is he tall? Regular of features? Does he possess the virtues of wisdom and justice? Truly, what is he like?"

The chief messenger leaned back in his chair, gazing at the fire. "Truly I am afraid I could not accurately tell you. He has a way of defying description. He is good. I know of none equal to him in strength, wisdom, and virtue. I am sorry to disappoint you regarding further details. I do know one thing, though, my lady," the chief messenger paused and gazed deeply into my eyes. "He will come when the time is right."

"What a strange gift he has sent me this time, though," I said to turn the conversation, maybe to glean useful knowledge. "I have never received a servant before—if that is her intended occupation, of course." I smiled. "You laugh, but in all sincerity, what am I to do with Mesda?"

"Mesda is here to be of service to you. Ask her, and she will best guide your course of action." He took one last draught from his wineglass, brushed a few remaining crumbs from his moustache and beard, and stood. "And now, if you will permit, we will depart for our chambers. Our road leads far, and we must embark at dawn."

"I will have my letter delivered to your chambers by morning, my lord."

He bowed, kissed my hand, and the company

departed.

In my room later that evening, I sat at my desk chewing a sharpened quill, my long hair already braided for bed. The letter from the son of the Mountain King, my intended one, lay open, the lines echoing of haunting love music. A slivered moon lingered outside my window.

...only know, sweet Judah, that you are loved...thoughts of you and your beauty fill my heart with joy, and although we are far apart at present, I eagerly await the day of our meeting...you are all fair, dear one...

I twirled the lovely words around, tasting each phrase like a delicacy, savoring my own thoughts. "Who are you?" I whispered. "What are you like? Does your person match written eloquence?" Sighing, I turned to the heavens, framed so ineptly by the window. "I have not even been told your name."

The torchlight did not sufficiently illuminate my desk, so I lit a candle and began.

"Dear Sir, I can only hope to convey the depth of my gratitude for the exquisite attention you have honored me with through your gifts and letter..." Why was it that my replies always sounded so cold? Dare I add, *"...and my greatest hope is that these are soon to be followed by the honor of your own presence"*? But the words of the messenger echoed still in my mind. *"I know one thing. He will come when the time is right."*

The hour was late when I at last sealed up an adequate letter, even if it did not fully contain what I wanted to say. A shake of a small gold bell by my desk brought the young servant who had been waiting outside to deliver my letter to the messenger. Alone again, I pulled out the box given me earlier that day, running my fingers along the delicate inlay. The box itself was a treasure, its beauty eclipsed only by the garment it held. A light glowed from the interior and the fabric shimmered in the candlelight when I held it aloft. What artistry, what perfection. Its wearer would be nothing short of radiant, worthy to walk among stars. Reverently, I touched the robe to my cheek, marveling at the soft texture. *This must be how a lamb feels.* Anna had tried to convince me to don the garment for the dinner, insisting I ought to "show off my beauty and get the word out about what the King's son was missing." I was sorely tempted. But, somehow, I knew that this was a robe of promise, not for wearing at the present time. Folding the gift with care, I hid the box in the back of my wardrobe and prepared for rest. Even if I could not wear it at this time, the robe was a much better gift than that odd old woman. Why would a king's son send me an old woman? And when would he make himself known, instead? But my eyelids proved heavier than these questions. I soon passed into the depths of slumber.

Dawn light filtering up the valley through the trees found me chatting in the courtyard with the chief messenger and his company as they made final preparations for their departure. It was a glorious day, without hint of clouds anywhere in the gray-orange sky.

"Again, thank you for honoring us with a visit, my lord. You are always welcome here."

"I thank you, sweet lady," Lord Gregory bowed. "I will bring your greetings to the Mountain King and his son without fail."

"Do you go there directly, then?"

"Not quite." He leaned closer, dropping his voice. "I do not wish to frighten you, my lady, but we have recently heard rumors of…stirrings in the southern lands."

I raised my eyebrows. "Any cause for alarm?"

"Perhaps not. We will investigate on our way, which will take us through a more circuitous route." He regarded me full in the face for a moment. "You may want to consider the same in the near future. Check the lower villages and farms. Keep your ears open."

"Thank you, sir," I nodded. "I will take that into consideration."

The sounds of bustling and shouts and joking were subsiding into the still moment that comes before the first step of any journey. The stable hands finished checking the horses' saddles and gear, and the head stableman approached. "M'lord, all is ready."

"Thank you." The man turned to me. "Remember, my lady, only send a messenger to the Mountain King and you will have all the help you ever need."

"Again, my thanks. May your journey be smooth and the sun bless your way."

"And blessings upon your road, my lady. I hope our paths may cross again soon. Until then—"

Hilda and Anna joined me as the company rode off down the village street, out the main gate, and down the valley toward the lower lands where the sun rose gloriously from the distant hills and spread its light to the ends of the earth.

I tore myself from the scene and spun toward the castle, my mind already made up. "Ladies, I have some business to attend to in the valley. Don't expect me until late tomorrow—possibly even until the following day."

At my words, Hilda stopped suddenly, her eyes wide. "My lady," Hilda seemed embarrassed. "I-I have a message from Mesda for you."

"Mesda? For me? How odd." I laughed. "All right, out with it—what does the woman want? New clothes?"

Hilda flushed deeper. "She sent a warning, saying that you should not go alone on your journey today. She advises you to take companions."

I'm sure my face betrayed surprise and irritation at this pronouncement—I couldn't help it. "*Advises* me? How very kind of her, I'm sure, to be so concerned." *That's all I need—a bossy, fussy old woman around the castle.* And how did she know about my plans? I only just made them this moment. I shrugged. Perhaps she had heard about the rumors already and made a lucky guess. "Anyway, I will be off within the hour or so."

"Alone, my lady?"

"Yes, alone." I grinned. "Don't worry. I will have my bow."

CHAPTER 4

My mare, Adara, tugged at my cloak while I leaned into her warm chest, my hands moving down her leg to her hoof. "Easy, love—yes, we are finally heading out together again." Satisfied with what I saw, I straightened and kissed her nose.

The head stableman loosely held the reins and beamed, his easygoing spirit a counterbalance to Adara's eager movements. "My lady, Adara should be as good as new. That lame foot healed up right smartly after we removed the thorn—a nasty one, it was."

"Thank you, Brunter. Your marvelous way with horses makes me believe sometimes that you can truly converse with them." I finished my inspection, getting nuzzled as I pulled straps and sneaked my beloved her sugar and carrots. "I really don't know how you do it."

"I think she knew she'd have to improve if she wanted to ride with her mistress again soon, my lady. That helped 'er along, for sure." Old Brunter grinned and patted Adara's golden neck affectionately. "She's a beauty, she is. Just like 'er mother."

"My own mother's glorious first horse," I whispered. I wanted to call this one Amia, after that beautiful place in the painting on my parents' wall, but my parents would not have it. Strange how they would not tell me why—or why they had to leave their old home.

"Her second," the groom corrected. "The sister of that horse was her first, and it was killed in the..." Brunter's voice trailed off, and he turned away. "I'm sorry, my lady."

"The Destruction? It's all right. Contrary to common belief, I can hear about it without much inner troubling. In fact," I laughed, "I believe I can reference the event with more ease than most of my elders, whether or not they had anything to do with the matter."

"We all had something to do with the matter," the elderly groom muttered almost under his breath.

I nodded for him to continue.

"What I mean to say is—" he paused, "even my own brother, the eldest—"

"Oh, Brunter. I'm sorry. Yes, yes, I see what you mean. You all lost someone in those times, at that place." I took the old man's hand. "I am sorry. I won't speak like that again."

He handed me the reins and smiled kindly. "No harm done, my lady."

I mounted Adara easily. On my horse—whom I'd befriended in girlhood—I had wings. "I will most likely not return until late tomorrow, or even the following day."

"I will be waiting." He bowed as Adara and I spun and cantered away.

Outside the gate, I gave Adara her head. The gallop felt wonderful, a release of pressured steam. We grew more refreshed rather than tired with the mad racing, flinging up dirt clumps and shattering morning dew to create a barely visible trail behind us. By the time we reached the lower part of the valley outside the castle walls, I was finally ready to slow down, ready for thinking. Adara instinctively veered left toward the forest, and I gave her free rein.

So much had happened since yesterday morning. That awkward gift, Mesda—what a surprise. Fortunately, both the head cook and the laundry mistress needed extra help, so the woman would be kept busy and out of my business. With that brief thought, I dismissed Mesda from my mind entirely. I had more pressing matters than an opinionated old woman.

What will happen with the lowlands of the south? I suppose I will discover more on the morrow, but if not… I shook that trailing idea away. My father taught me that worrying accomplishes nothing. On the contrary, if I was honest with myself, I almost hoped that a skirmish of sorts might be in the making. What a chance to finally prove myself capable and worthy as a leader. My mother had, of course, trained me prodigiously in the skills of archery and sword fighting as a proper warrior. My father had added a keen knowledge of tracking and the ways of nature, how to read the woods and ground and sky. As thick branches darkened the path, Adara's rhythmic hoofbeats drummed my mind into dreamlike scenes of battle and glory. I saw myself, sword and voice raised high in splendor and battle cries, Adara leading the charge with speed and strength of fire…

Adara's sudden startle jolted me from the reverie. With one motion, I drew my bow and nocked an arrow. Too late.

A row of men stood facing me, their hands gripping what must be sword hilts behind their cloaks.

I aimed at the tallest man. *I am not yet defeated.* "Do not move."

"It is you who should not move, I think," said the man, taking a step forward.

"Another step, and I send this through your brain."

"Alas, my lady," the man smiled, "if you were to turn, you would find five arrows ready to fly." He gave a small signal, and the men and women who had quietly surrounded me from the back moved slowly around to the front. I lowered my bow.

"There is no need to call the alarm, my lady," the man said, catching the thought in my eye before I could seize the horn hanging on my shoulder. "We intend you no harm. Indeed, do not be afraid."

"If that is true," I nudged Adara to back away, "then who are you?"

The man unhooked the front of his deep green cloak and let it fall, revealing the telltale blue and white of the people of the Mountain King. My breath caught, and I immediately reined in Adara. "I don't understand."

All weapons were now lowered, and smiles flashed around. The man who was obviously the leader bowed. "My lady, we have been sent by the

Mountain King to ensure that you abide in safety. We live throughout the land, and we keep an eye on everything, ready for orders from the palace."

"I have never seen you before, nor heard tell of you."

"We are only seen when we wish to be seen or when commanded to reveal ourselves."

"But who…" I suddenly understood. "Did the envoy from the Mountain King pass through here earlier? Was it they who told you I would be coming and ordered you to reveal your presence to me?"

The man nodded.

No wonder the company had decided to take a more circuitous route home. "I assume correctly, then, that you were the ones from whom they expected to hear more about certain…*rumors*?"

Again, a nod. "Of unrest in the south? Yes."

"And you will tell me news? You will confirm the verity of the rumors?"

"Yes, and no, I'm sorry to say. Our scouts in the south have passed along information that the attitude is perceptibly negative toward this realm at present, and their information is always accurate. However, they do not have access to the inner planning of the ruler of the south." Here he appeared serious. "There is a man, though, in the southern reaches of this kingdom, who has certain…shall we say, connections, and he may know more than we at present."

"And why have you not communicated with this man yourself?"

"We have been instructed to not do so."

I raised an eyebrow. "If the man is the one whom I know of in those parts…"

"Yes, it is he of whom we speak, and danger is not our reason for avoiding the man." He cleared his throat. "My lady, we have been instructed to leave that particular connection to you."

I did not even try to mask my astonishment. "Well, then." I shifted. "I ought to be going. It is a long ride to the village Naphtrona before dark and then another half day's ride to my destination."

"One more word, my lady." He stepped closer and lowered his voice.

"Yes?"

"Whatever tale you hear from your contact in the south—remember, the Mountain King is ever ready to aid you. Send word to us here. A whispered message, and you will receive anything you have need of in the coming days."

I nodded. "Thank you for your concern. However," I straightened my shoulders, "I believe I will manage to find a useful solution to any problems that may arise." I turned Adara to the forest road. "Farewell."

The people bowed gracefully. When I glanced at the road behind a moment later, not a trace of anyone could be seen.

~*~

The bed that night was lumpy in places, but I settled in as best I could. The innkeepers in Naphtrona, a kind couple, had fussed over me. My stomach groaned from the abundance of cakes, wine, meat, and warm bread. The couple's well-intentioned flurrying resulted in a profusion of overstuffed goose pillows, hurriedly-cut flowers, and at least three garish rugs scattered at random in my room. A small fire provided timely warmth. I had noticed signs in the sky—the weather was changing, the wind cutting suddenly across the plains. My window stayed tightly closed that night.

I planned to leave before dawn. Meanwhile, the ceiling was my only companion as sleep eluded me. *Why does the Mountain King insist on treating me as one who is incapable? Should I not have the freedom to do as I like, to meet the success or failure that is my lot? Must I be protected as a babe, merely because I am betrothed to his son?* Memories of my parents flooded forth, and I sank gratefully into the familiar images. Strong, capable, noble—there was nothing they were unable to do, I was sure of it. Yes, there had been stories of an epic failure during their rule tied to the Destruction, but what of it in the grand scheme of things? They had brought peace and prosperity to the kingdom. Surely, all rulers make mistakes at some point. I did not fear failure.

There was one thing I was determined *not* to do, regardless of tomorrow's news. I would not ask for help from the Mountain King.

CHAPTER 5

My hands chafed on the reins—if only I had packed Hilda's soothing balm. The ride was wilder than I had anticipated. Wind whipped across the plains at speeds swifter than woman and horse could ride. Adara's ears pinned back. Erratic gusts wreaked havoc on her mane, but nothing could impede her powerful strides. The smell of an incoming storm blew by, and we were driven even faster.

A few short stops for water were all that I allowed, and in fact, Adara seemed as eager to continue as was her mistress. Time was short, but nothing could condense the distance to our destination. Now and again, we passed people hurrying down the road. I imagined the travelers watched in surprise and awe as a young woman on a golden horse thundered past. Eventually, my daydreaming expanded to include armor, a sword, and a legion of warriors courageously following their leader to battle. Phantom armies charged, and I led the way as my people beat back the enemy. In my mind, I raised the shield of my father in triumph before riding victoriously to Marah.

A spray of icy water jerked me back as Adara pounded through a shallow stream. "Easy on the rocks, girl." But she shook her mane with an eager cry, flicking droplets over my laughing face and aching hands. No obstacle seemed to faze Adara.

Grumwold had always taught me that difficulties were opportunities for growth. Could I not turn this trying circumstance into something that brought good? Could this be the opportunity to establish my worth as governor? *Those may have been mere dreams of battle, but I can save my people from invaders and prove myself worthy of my parents' and Grumwold's legacies. And perhaps…* I gripped the reins tighter, *…perhaps my claiming the rights of savior of my people will entice my betrothed himself down from his mountain stronghold.* My aching hands were forgotten. The way to honor and glory lay clear before me in this terrible opportunity of southern rebellion. *Lady Judah, daughter of Lord Leo and Lady Elanna, bold, independent governor, warrior with the spirit and the rights of a conqueror.* I smiled.

It was midday by the time I dismounted at my destination, a small border town that did not boast much beyond an exceptionally clear well and an overabundance of dust. How the two managed to cohabit, I couldn't imagine, but I gratefully drank from the former while brushing the latter off my sweaty mare. After paying well for a stable boy to care for Adara, I set out to a house on the edge of town where my contact could be found. He was an old gentleman, once an unobtrusive servant of my parents after they settled in Castle Marah. He moved to this border town while I was still a little girl, and my parents used his unique observation skills to keep informed of the various goings-on of the kingdom.

I pounded on the door with the signal of my parents. Several minutes passed. The wind was growing stronger, brushing my eyelashes with dust, pulling at the hair I had so firmly braided back, whipping at my riding skirt. Somewhere out of sight, eyes were watching my every move. I could feel it. Finally, the chink of several locks rent the uneasy silence. The door swung open.

"I know why you have come." Even with the tremor of age, the voice that greeted me was forceful. "Please sit—there is much to say, and yes, time is short."

~*~

The wind shook the stable's walls in its growing fury, and I noted gathering clouds with some consternation. The stable boy, smiling and chatty, gripped the lead in one hand and swung a small sack in the other as he brought out Adara from the stable. He had taken care to brush my beautiful horse until her coat glowed. "The storm should be an exciting one, my lady."

I nodded politely while checking the saddle straps and bridle. Now was not the time to think about the news I had just received. Only speed mattered, and it was time to take some risks. I examined Adara's healed hoof. Good—still strong. The boy chuckled. "I've had such an odd feelin' this whole time that I should know who you are, my lady, but try as I might, I just can't figure out why." He paused, but when no reply was forthcoming, he continued talking. "Ah, well. Your steed is the most magnificent I've ever cared for, she is, and I'll at least sleep tonight knowing I've done my best for the both of you." He slipped the horse one more handful of grain before untying the rope. He was obviously infatuated with my mare. How did Adara always seem to have this effect on people? If she were a person, I would have set her up in politics. Adara pricked her ears forward and nudged him gently. Splendid animal. "I hope you will not get caught in the storm, beautiful one," the boy whispered as he stroked her nose.

"I think my horse likes you," I broke in with a smile. "She can be a wonderful conversationalist." A deep blush swallowed the boy's many freckles, and he turned away to pick up a bucket.

As Adara drank, I scanned the sky again while fighting to keep my hair tucked out of the wind's reach. It was going to be close. If I rode hard, if Adara was up for it, I could make it back, at the very least, to a village inn a few hours south of the castle. From there, a messenger could let my people know of my whereabouts.

"Is my lady planning to ride far? You are not from these parts?" The stable boy's face scrunched as he handed me the reins.

"I'm afraid so, and no, I'm not from here." I rubbed Adara's shoulder and adjusted the saddle bag. "My deep appreciation, boy, for your excellent care of my horse." I put a gold piece in his hand and mounted my steed.

The boy's gaping eyes tore from the coin to look up at me. "But—forgive my boldness, my lady—the weather—"

"I might get a little wet." I laughed. "But I trust I will find myself more than a match for whatever may come my way."

The boy bit his lip and bowed. "May your journey be blessed, my lady."

"I thank you." I whispered in Adara's ear, and then we were off like the lightning streaking the southern horizon.

Adara must have rested and eaten well, for she seemed as eager for a gallop across the plains as her mistress. So united were woman and horse that we flew almost as a single being. If anyone else had dared to journey in this weather, they would have been treated to a regal vision. However, other travelers must have wisely remained where they were, for the wind rushed across the plains, pulling storm clouds in their fury, whipping the grasses until it seemed they would fly out of the earth altogether. We saw no one. My heart pounded in sync with Adara's hooves in the mad dash toward home, and my mind flew with equal fury through the events of that afternoon.

My contact had proved as useful as I had hoped. His words—whispered, fast—chilled my very breath. Could this be happening? But his tale withstood careful questioning and cross-examination. Even more importantly, his hands had told the truth. This was something that Grumwold had taught me.

"How do you know when someone is telling the

truth, Grumwold? Is it in their eyes?" I had asked.

"Child, the truth can be in the eyes, but some have learned the art of lying so well that their eyes are as their mouths."

"Then what is a person to do?"

"I have found, dear Judah, that truth never fails to speak through hands. Watch the hands—their muscles for tension, their fingers for nervous ticks, watch for sweat and color and limpness. When you need to know if someone speaks truth to you, see their eyes, but do not lose sight of their hands."

My contact's eyes and hands spoke truth. And so I flew with speed and recklessness toward home. Time called for action. This was my time; I was sure of it.

A vision of my mother suddenly rose before me. Strong, beautiful, courageous—Elanna had been everything I aspired to be. Imagining Elanna at the height of her youth, fighting bravely, reigning wisely, leading with grace and confidence had always inspired me to do my best, to drive to the limit and then push myself further. My father, too, moved me to action. I had loved going with him on expeditions to the woods and plains to learn the ways of the earth. Both parents taught me to be strong and trained me to rule well in their place when the time came.

But as always, questions blanketed memories. Why did they always wear black? What were they hiding? My parents, beautiful even in their old age, had worn black for as long as I could remember. Elderly servants from Amia said my parents had started this custom after the Destruction, when they left for their new home. They could not—or would not? —tell me why. My questions and pleadings were merely met with quiet, sad smiles and answers that did not say much.

I wondered if their personalities changed when they left Amia. Were they always so wistful with a secret sorrow? Was it because they were in the Destruction? *I must ask Grum*—but Grumwold's permanent absence stopped me short. She would not be able to answer this question. But were there answers to be found elsewhere—old documents, letters? *Perhaps a clue hides in the records of the castle.* Adara abruptly slowed, warning me that she was about to jump a stream. It was getting difficult to see. Storm clouds had quickly enveloped us, and we faced a dark, deserted plain hemmed by forest, with no welcoming lights of a village in sight.

Adara's nostrils flared and she shied, twitching her ears. Then thunder roared through the heavens, and she hurdled forward, racing the wind. The weight of the sky threatened to crush us, giant black fists pressing toward earth, hunting the unprotected. Lightning shattered darkness, and again, thunder hounded us. I had to scream now for Adara to hear me. We reached the tree line in a few minutes, although we were not really any safer. Great, blinding lightning bolts jarred my very bones.

I sensed Adara's growing panic. Could I maintain control of my own wits? *Be strong.* "Hold steady, girl." Could Adara even hear me? My own terror rose like a spectral when my sight all but disappeared in the storm's endless, howling darkness.

Then came the rain.

A shattering crack rent the air—a flash of light, a sharp pain, and everything went black.

CHAPTER 6

Whispers. Lights, too many lights. So much heat. Cold. Deep, deep cold. Where was I? Something wet and nasty smelling lay on my forehead. I tried to brush it off. A sudden lightning pain shot through my head, and I cried out.

"It's all right, dearie. It's all right. No need to move." Someone tucked my arm in and adjusted whatever was on my head. Then the voices faded out, and all was dark.

Three days passed, and then a few more before I fully woke. The elderly doctors, a couple who had together learned medicine arts, stayed incessantly by my side. Their smiles and joyful cries at my smallest movements surely encouraged all who hovered like so many worried pigeons. Thankfully, the room was mostly empty when I awoke. I shivered uncontrollably for a minute. My head felt like fire.

"Shh…shh…it's all right." The old woman finished placing a fresh poultice over my head. She tucked another blanket around my sides. "You've had quite a bump, you have."

I blinked. Even the slivers of light bursting through the closed curtains drove like needles into my brain. "Where—where—"

"In your own bedroom, dearie," the old woman interrupted. "Now, hold still while I adjust this thing."

It took all my power to not cry out. I dug a fingernail into my palm, but none of my limbs seemed able to move. "What happened?"

"You had a bit of a fall," a deeper voice broke in. "It's important that you rest."

A young girl entered, bearing a bowl of steaming water. She stared wide-eyed at me, and then trotted out of the room when the old woman gave her a gentle nudge. *What? Who? Why can't I move?* Questions and thundering pain coagulated into a panic that choked me. Tears spilled, catching in my ears on the way down.

"There, there, now. Don't you be upsetting yourself, dearie. Me and my husband know what we're up to, and we were here before to help your dear parents." The old woman's wrinkled smile and carefully twisted white hair were vaguely familiar. Her voice, reassuring and kind, gave me strength, and I breathed again. The physicians. This couple had tended my parents.

"And don't worry, my dear," the husband piped in, patting my hand. "Your horse is safe and well."

"She stayed with you the whole time." The wife seemed pleased, as if she had arranged the entire thing herself.

My horse? A jumble of memory flew to their places. The contact. A wild ride. Lightning. I saw as if in slow motion what had happened. My breath froze.

"How long have I been…?"

"Asleep? Ages, my lady, just ages." Anna and Hilda hovered beside me. "You had us worried sick."

"You left on your journey about a week ago."

"You scared us beyond belief."

"Ladies." The doctor's voice was impressively stern. "You are wearying our patient." He pointed firmly toward the door.

"But—"

"No and no. Shoo, shoo." With great sighs and several secret, undecipherable signs and winks to me, Anna and Hilda left the room in its silent watchfulness.

"Has it really been a week?"

The doctors had to lean in closely to hear.

"Give or take a little. But don't you worry, dearie. You have been resting, and that is exactly what your body needs." The old woman readjusted my bedsheets for the hundredth time. This doctor was apparently a great believer in the healing power of tight bedsheets, which partly accounted for my inability to move. Was I supposed to remember something? Was there something I needed to do?

I drifted off again.

When I awoke, a bowl of hot broth sat by my head. I submitted to being fed as a child without complaining, delighting my doctors by not only finishing the bowl, but also asking for more. "Am I very ill, doctors?"

The wife smiled a little and touched my arm. "Well, you did get quite the bump on your head from the tree branch and falling from your horse."

"But is there more than that?" I gazed from one to the other.

They exchanged glances, and then the husband spoke after his wife nodded. "There is a fever, one that does not seem quite…regular. It worries us a little. You may not have noticed, but it is quite present."

At this moment, Anna and Hilda tiptoed in, and this time the doctors seemed to welcome the distraction. They nodded and moved away.

"Oh, my lady, we have been so worried. When we saw your head wound—and then the doctors told us about the fever and everything—" Anna burst into tears. Hilda patted her hand and raised her eyes as if imploring for patience. "Sorry, my lady. It's just been so awful."

Did they think I was even now at death's door? I attempted to move my head, but a sharp pain quickly halted that effort. "What exactly happened? I remember riding Adara in a storm, but that is all."

Whatever Anna was about to say drowned in her throat as Hilda clapped her hand over Anna's mouth. "What a dramatic day it was." Hilda's voice dropped like a curtain. Anna may have been the actress, but Hilda was the storyteller. "It was late, and we could see a storm forming over the plains. We hoped you had chosen to remain in a village inn for another night. No word came, however, which was unusual, so we became very worried. We were ready to send out a search party if we didn't hear from you by morning. Early, though it was still dark out, a pounding cry on the castle gates brought us all out in a hurry." Another pause, either for dramatic effect or to stifle Anna's attempt to jump in. Hilda glared at her friend and continued. "There you were, covered in blood, on a makeshift stretcher carried by a whole group of men." She shivered for a moment. Her eyes suddenly twinkled. "If it hadn't been so horrible, it would have been most exciting."

Anna sniffed and wiped her eyes. "Some of the men were rather cute."

I waved my hand. "But these men who carried me here—who were they? Where were they from?"

"I'm not sure who they were, but I have an idea of where they were from." Hilda leaned forward in a conspiratorial whisper. "They all wore long, dark green cloaks, but I glimpsed blue and white tunics underneath. You know what that means. They came from the Mountain King."

A groan erupted from my throat at the mention of the cloaks and colors.

"My lady?" Hilda touched my hand. "Is the pain very bad, my lady?"

"It's not that, it's—" I sighed. So much for doing things without the help of the Mountain King. "Nothing. How interesting. How did they find me? Carry on."

"They said they came upon you on the ground, Adara protecting you. It was raining so horribly, and that wind—" Hilda's face suddenly twisted up as if she were trying to hold back tears, and Anna started to sniffle. "You were bleeding something awful. They were not sure how long you had been like that."

"You could have died," Anna burst out, and Hilda shushed her.

Anna glanced around, perhaps checking if the physicians were out of hearing range. "And you still are in grave danger, my lady," she whispered. "These doctors do not seem to be able to heal this treacherous fever, and I worry—" she started to cry again, "we may be running out of time."

There it was again—that choking panic. I closed my eyes, counting to ten and taking deep breaths until my heartrate slowed. "But these are the best doctors in the kingdom."

Anna leaned closer. Even Hilda leaned in. "There are physicians in other kingdoms, wise people who practice healing arts in ways our doctors never learned. I hear rumors of one great man in particular who is able to heal all ills." She smiled and laughed theatrically as the physicians turned our way, and then she grew serious again. "They call him the Enlightened One."

I raised my eyebrow. "I heard his name mentioned in passing once, but I do not know much beyond his rumored powers and political connections."

Politics. *That's right. The news from the south.* How could I have forgotten?

I motioned to them. "Anna. Hilda. I have to get up. I must do something immediately."

Anna fussed momentarily with my bowl of soup, probably hoping to not arouse further suspicion from the doctors.

"You have heard something?" Hilda whispered.

The ladies were well aware of their privileged position. They knew that anything passing my lips at this time was to be held in the strictest confidence.

"Yes—my contact in the south confirmed the rumor." Hilda seemed alarmed and glanced at my hands, which were beginning to tremble. "Not just one, but three southern kingdoms are conspiring against our land. If we are to do anything to defend ourselves, we must act immediately. We must—" I felt my eyes roll back as the room flickered. The last thing I heard was shrieking and the shattering of a soup bowl.

~*~

That evening, I have been told, darkness enveloped a palace high in the clouds. There was no moon that night. The time was right. A figure, cloaked and silent, turned back to grasp strong hands that stretched out to him from within the doorway.

The Mountain King had known this day would come. The day he would send his only son to the valley and to the people below. He was their king. But they did not know his son.

What I do not know is if the king wept as he bid his son farewell? Mention was made that the son set his face like flint. He had to save his beloved, even though I had rejected the king's help.

The one who told me said that if the moon had shone, it would have revealed love, sorrow, resolve in a look between the Mountain King and his son. A final handgrip, and the son was gone. Rhythmic hoofbeats disappeared down the road from the mountain palace, and a single bright star thrust through the clouds to flash a greeting or blessing. The piercing eyes of the Mountain King followed as his only son tore into the night. Finally, the king turned and closed the door behind him, leaving only the gleaming star to watch and wait.

CHAPTER 7

It had reached outside the castle walls. I had hoped it would take longer than it did.

The single spark that spreads faster in a castle than fire or plague is *rumor*. This is a well-known fact. And the rumors that now flew along corridors and up and down village streets out to the farmlands were particularly frightening.

How big was the invading army? Five kingdoms? Ten kingdoms?

We are planning to attack.

We are not planning to attack.

Up and down, the rumors spread. I discovered later that people in the valley had started locking their doors at night. Castle dwellers hid their valuables. According to rumor, folks glared suspiciously at every stranger. Everyone was disquieted. It was as though above Castle Marah fluttered the tattered remnants of peace, a flag of despair.

Finally, the rumors made their way to my sickroom. Hilda happened to be in with me when they came. The servant collecting the laundry asked the servant washing the floor a few ill-timed questions: when did she believe the southern invasion would take place? And would she join the army if things came to that? The questions reverberated around the silent room. Hilda took one look at my bulging eyes and shoved both servants through the doorway. She knew me well enough, I'm sure, to accurately predict that the rising temperature of my initial shock would plummet to below freezing within seconds.

The door had barely closed when my icy voice struck her back. "Hilda."

She flinched. "My lady?"

"Please be so good as to ring for Anna. I have something to say to you."

Anna must have known what had happened the moment she saw my face. She sighed, raised her hands in mute appeal to the ceiling, and plopped next to the sickbed. I coldly indicated for Hilda to take the seat next to Anna.

"What," I began, "is the meaning of all this?" Icicles hung from my words.

Anna attempted to smile in a ghastly, sheepish grimace. "The meaning of what?"

The room temperature dropped lower. "The invasion. The one that no one knows about. The one that is a strictly confidential, dangerous secret?"

I will not relay the conversation in its entirety.

I chewed Anna and Hilda up and down, the worst of the few comparable times in our shared history.

Anna and Hilda protested their innocence. That is, Hilda protested their innocence. Anna sobbed.

"But then how can this be accounted for? The words I whispered to you in this room are now the prattle of idle tongues in every marketplace from here to kingdom's end." The heat of my wrath hovered in the air, palpable and heavy.

Hilda glanced at Anna.

She avoided her eyes, suddenly showing intense interest in a loose thread.

"What is it?" I demanded. "Speak."

"Well, my lady…You have been very ill, you know. Feverish…" Hilda twisted her skirt in her hands, refusing to make eye contact. "I'm afraid you may have started the rumors yourself," she muttered, reddening.

I fell back on my pillows. "No." *How could this be?* "Did I—did I speak state secrets in…delirium?"

"Rather loudly, actually," Anna picked up in a whisper. "I'm afraid you quite shouted at times."

Hilda touched my arm. "We did what we could to hush, but…"

"It was too late," I finished quietly. "So you were not surprised when I spoke with you about what I learned?"

"No." Anna and Hilda quickly shushed my apology for doubting their loyalty. Hilda pointed out that my assumption was only logical. Anna said she would have thought the same thing. Hilda also hinted delicately that, although she may be far from perfect, she hoped I knew she is not a blathering fool. In short, the ladies did what they could to calm me, but the physicians had to give me a sedative to sleep that night.

The following day brought news that my advisors deemed important enough to disturb me. Villagers and farmers alike had gathered in a panic in Marah demanding answers about a massive army from the south. The people insisted on reassurance from the governor herself.

Anna declared that she was going to have hysterics about "the mob upon our very doorstep," so Hilda sent her away with a cup of tea after escorting in the advisors.

I almost laughed at their discomfiture.

The tallest advisor spoke first. "Ahem. My lady. We bring news of an…unpleasant nature."

"Some issues of civil…instability." Those in attendance shuffled their feet.

"Perhaps," the man stared at the floor, "one might go so far as to term it *civil unrest*."

"Are you referring to the massive throng that has congregated outside?" I finally broke in. "I can hear the shouts from here."

Like a rupturing dam, the advisors all spoke at once, pouring out concerns, fears, suggestions. Remarkably, the discussion sparked the first bit of energy I had felt in a long time, and I sat up straighter, speaking more like myself. The advisors seemed pleased and told me they would send news to the people that their governor was on the mend.

But the people refused to leave. Instead, they set up a sort of camp siege while they waited to hear from me.

Meanwhile, the doctors prepared to go home, content with my now steady progress. They gave Anna and Hilda a strict series of instructions about giving medications for the fever, bed rest, and informing them of any changes. Then they departed.

Anna, who had frequently said how disgusted she was that the doctors were unable to get rid of the fever entirely, seized this opportunity to beg me again to send for the Enlightened One. "He can help you. He can completely heal you. I am sure of it." Anna paced the room like a curly-haired panther. "Things are getting out of hand around here. We need you. You need to be healed now."

Hilda rolled her eyes and continued to organize the medications. "Anna, really. Must you always be so dramatic?"

Anna ignored her. Clasping my hands and dropping to her knees in front of me, she cried out, "Promise me. Promise you'll at least consider my suggestion."

I laughed. "I promise I'll consider it, dear heart, but do get up. You nearly overturned my soup."

But the strain of trying to solve the kingdom's problems from my bed quickly pushed the thought right out of my mind. The days were further complicated by the string of visitors who came to extend their sympathy to me for my illness and wish me well.

One visitor brought me both surprise and agitation. Soon after the physicians left, Hilda came in with an apologetic smile. "My lady, the servant Mesda requests a short audience with you. She is waiting outside."

Anna rolled her eyes and huffed.

I frowned. "Mesda? That odd servant woman? She wants to see me?" I sighed. "I suppose you must send her in, too."

Mesda had been a rather ugly, old woman when she arrived, but she was now yet older and uglier, even sickly and weak. She slowly shuffled in and bowed her head respectfully, bent over in what I guessed was arthritic pain exacerbated by her labor at the castle.

Trying to mask my astonishment and—what was it? Guilt? —I quickly said, "You wished to see me?"

"Ay, my lady. I have a private message for you." She gazed pointedly at Anna, who hovered nearby exuding disgust.

"A moment, please, Anna," I requested, nodding toward the door.

Anna raised her eyebrows even farther and flounced off, the perfect impression of a princess insulted by the sight of a toad.

"My lady, the time is now," Mesda said in her croaky voice when the door closed. "It is time to call for the aid of the Mountain King. He and his son wish it."

A lightning bolt striking the floor at this moment could not have sparked greater shock. How did this woman receive messages from the Mountain King? Perhaps she was connected to those silent watchers in the forest. *She is probably making this up. Or, even more likely, she's growing delusional in her old age.*

I squirmed. "Oh, ah, how nice of them to offer. Please give them my thanks, I'm sure, and tell them I'll consider their kind proposition."

Mesda was frail, but she was sharp as an arrow tip. She leaned forward, her eyes piercing. "My lady, this message is in earnest. I am not playing with you. Accept the help of the Mountain King."

I felt my face redden. "And, pray tell, why must I do every wish of the Mountain King? Why may I not follow the advice of my own heart and the words of my advisors? Why must I abstain from proving my own worth and strength and ask instead for help when I'm sure that the Mountain King himself would rather be pleased with my taking initiative and action?"

"The Mountain King and his son wish it," Mesda repeated.

"I thank you for your concern." I rang a bell for a rather malicious-looking Anna to escort Mesda from the room.

The old woman turned to go but twisted back for a moment to point her gnarled finger directly at me. "Do not forget," she rasped. "Call on the Mountain King for help." She folded her hands in a final supplication and then submitted to Anna's hand on her elbow.

"You old witch, don't you know better than to disturb your mistress with your wild claims?" Anna hissed, barely lowering her voice. "Your silence serves better than your words."

Mesda peered calmly back at her. "You would do well, young one, to heed the message yourself." She turned and hobbled her way down the corridor, leaving Anna glaring behind her.

Anna stomped out, presumably to make sure the old woman did not return.

Reentering the room a few minutes later, Anna gasped.

I was rising to dress, pale and leaning on Hilda's arm like a crutch. "My lady, what on earth?"

"I will be fine, Anna." I strained as I regained balance after being mainly bedridden for a few weeks. "I must go and speak to the people before they actually become a mob."

"Has that old hag driven you to this?" Anna demanded.

I laughed. "No, dear, but I do happen to hear the shouting of many voices outside the window. Don't you?" I slowly sat down again to have my hair dressed by Anna as Hilda fetched my shoes and rouged my face. "I must speak to the people. They need their governor to lead now."

"I'm sure they could wait a few more days," Anna grumbled under her breath, but she continued to braid and pin up my hair.

I am sure my tight lips bespoke my determination, for the ladies did not protest any further. As soon as I was satisfied with my appearance, I allowed Anna and Hilda to support my arms as I made my way to the platform in the village square.

The village was crowded. The number of people camping in and around Marah had grown steadily each day as delegates from around the kingdom arrived for news they could report back to their countrymen. I sent a messenger ahead to announce that I was coming.

The mass of people packed into the square was

almost difficult to believe. A sense of expectant urgency crackled in the air. When I climbed the platform steps, supported by Anna and Hilda and flanked by my advisors, a great cheer went up as if a fire had been sparked. The stream of messages, food, and gifts that had flooded the castle testified that the people trusted and loved me, and they worried to hear of my illness. Deeply moved at the scene, it took all my willpower to not tear up as we settled on the platform.

At a sign, the people went silent.

"My people," I began, "I thank you for coming. I thank you for your support and love during my illness. You have proved yourselves strong for me, and now, I intend to prove myself strong for you." Sweat dripped down my forehead from the effort.

I knew my attendants stood ready to catch me if needed.

My words, at first quiet and uncertain, gained in strength and volume as I continued speaking. I drew strength from my people. I could almost feel hope rise as I poured forth from my heart. Yes, an army, comprised of three kingdoms, was preparing an invasion sometime in the not-too-distant future. No, I was not going to waver in the face of adversity. I—we—were mighty together, and together we would prepare, we would unite, and when the time came, we would fight. Cheers rose high to the heavens at this point, and the advisors struggled to quiet the crowd so that I could finish. I thanked them for being here, for showing their support and concern, and I urged them to take courage. "Go home now," I said, "and give boldness to our brothers and sisters. Tell them we will be ready. Together, we will prevail. Go home now, and watch—I will send messengers within the week with instructions. Be ready, my people, and thank you, from the depths of my heart. Thank you."

The last words were almost lost in the roar of approval and applause that followed. I continued to smile bravely, but I grabbed for Hilda's and Anna's arms and briefly stumbled as I stepped back. The fever throbbed in my temples.

My attendants almost carried me back to my bed.

"You should not have done that, my lady," Hilda chided gently. "You are not fully recovered, and you really must be careful. However," she tucked me in bed and helped Anna undo my hair, "that was beautifully said. You put heart back into the people."

I weakly smiled and drifted to sleep.

The following morning, I met with my advisors in the council room. The advisors first urged me to call for the aid of the Mountain King, but I refused.

Since I would not call for help, they counseled me to immediately raise up an army from among the people as they did not know how much time would pass before an invasion would begin. This I agreed to do.

The next day, I watched from the great window in my bedchamber as riders flew in all directions with detailed instructions for the village heads, who were to gather recruits, elect captains, and start training local units for war. Additionally, all able-bodied citizens were to build fortifications and prepare weapons.

Everyone was to help with hiding food stashes for times of need and in case of siege.

"We can do this," I whispered to myself over and over, willing it to be true. "The people are determined and resourceful. We can do this. I can do this." Exhausted, I prayed I was right.

Perhaps through sheer strength of will, I began to improve rapidly. Although the fever still held its grip on me, I began to look almost well and walked slowly among the villagers on Hilda's arm, offering encouragement and praise. I knew the visible presence of the governor gave strength to the hearts and hands of my people. Like a disturbed anthill, the whole kingdom whirred with activity. The only thing that could have thrilled me more was the news that came abruptly one afternoon as I woke from my nap.

"My lady." Hilda rushed in, grinning, face flushed. "We hear rumors that have only now been confirmed." She saw my face and laughed. "Not to worry, my lady. This is good news. People from the eastern side of the kingdom have reported," she paused with dramatic effect, "that the shepherds have returned to the land."

My jaw dropped.

Hilda laughed and danced like a jester. "Even better, rumors say eventually some may come here to Marah."

CHAPTER 8

Marking off another day on my calendar, I sighed and crawled into bed. It had become a habit, this lying awake for hours, staring at the ceiling and untangling a web from my mind to the future. Weeks had passed since my accident. The days marched on, and my people's determination never wavered. It became apparent over time, however, that sheer willpower and courage would not be enough. We were not equal to fighting off the forces that were slowly preparing against our land. Spies came back to report on the size, weaponry, and skill of the enemy armies. It was obvious that my small country would be no match for them. The people began to lose their courage, but I did not. I was, however, dismayed, and my hope waned further with every day.

The fever, although low and controlled through medication, also refused to relinquish its hold. Turning over, I sighed again. An image of Anna arose, and I blinked. My redheaded attendant had made me promise to consider consulting a wise healer…the Enlightened One. Others had joined Anna in urging me to contact the Enlightened One since I would not apply to the Mountain King for aid. Anna regularly brought stories from the castle library to show me that even the strongest rulers in history sought help when needed. "Surely, my lady, using one's resources is not a sign of weakness?" she pleaded. "Calling on the Enlightened One would be just that.."

Sitting up, I grabbed the herbal tea that sat, now cold, near my bed. Perhaps she was right. I swallowed the tea's bitterness in a gulp. I didn't have any prior relationship with this so-called Enlightened One, unlike with the Mountain King. Maybe it would be foolish to not use his medical advice and reported wisdom. Resolving to give the matter additional consideration, I slipped into a restless sleep.

But my spies' reports soon shoved those ideas far from my mind.

The council members and I sat silent for a long time after the devastating news. My neck throbbed. I knew what I had to say. People always told me I looked especially like my mother had at times like this, when I was resolved to do something.

"We will work harder." Unasked questions hovered on the lips of those at the table with me. "We must. I will go—" but Hilda interrupted me, tiptoeing in and whispering in my ear.

"Must I really?" My cheeks burned.

"They say she has mere minutes, my lady," Hilda replied.

I sighed. "Please excuse me."

Surprised murmurs pursued me.

Hilda led the way down to the lower levels of the castle where servants labored. At the far end, sprouting off a long hallway like leaves were small rooms that provided quarters for the lower servants. The farthest, smallest, and darkest room—more a cell than a room—had been granted at her request to the old woman who now lay dying.

"Mesda," I took the old woman's gnarled hands. How odd. Her fingers were stained black, as with ink. I perched on a rickety wooden stool. A rough table stood like an ancient sentry near the cot. "I am sorry that you are ill." I stared, uneasy, into the face of the dying, trying to ignore the guilt pricking my conscience. Was I somehow to blame for her poor condition?

"I will not survive the hour, my lady, but do not be sorry—I have completed my final task," Mesda whispered, her voice raspy. Despite the tone, the woman's words rang with grace and dignity. She opened her eyes—bright blue and clear—to focus on my face. "The Master and his son love you, my lady." Coughing forced her to pause.

I blushed at this reference to my betrothed.

The spasm finally passed, and she continued. "He wants you to ask for his help."

Angry heat boiled up as if a chasm had wrenched open in my heart, threatening to engulf me in a wave of fire. What right did this person have to intrude on my personal affairs? My relationship with the Mountain King and his son was no business of hers. But the suffering in this old woman's final minutes were water to flame, and I paused. "Thank you, Mesda."

"You will ask him?" she whispered.

It was tempting to lie to the dying woman. But I suspected that Mesda would read the truth in my eyes. "No. I will not."

A tear that ran down the wrinkled face cracked my heart anew, but this time springs of compassion flowed out. I leaned over and kissed the old woman's pale cheek. Then it was time to leave. Passing Hilda in the doorway, I murmured, "Will you?"

Hilda nodded.

"Thank you. No one should die alone." I went out.

Resting later in an armchair by the fire, I rubbed my forehead, wrestling with uneasiness. "Why, she's only an old serving woman, after all." The angry words flew out, hot and ugly. What was wrong with me? It had to be the wretched fever. I grabbed a piece of unfinished embroidery and then threw it down again.

A knock on the door interrupted my misery. "Come in," I snapped.

Hilda rushed in, wide-eyed and gasping.

"Hilda. What is the matter? Has she passed?"

Hilda nodded.

"Has it upset you? What is wrong? You are making me nervous." My temples pounded.

"I am sorry, my lady," Hilda trembled violently. "But the strangest thing has happened. I can hardly believe it."

I gently pulled Hilda's hands from her face. "What is it?"

Hilda took several deep breaths. "After you left, I sat down with Mesda and tried to make her comfortable. She wanted me to lean closer, since she was fast fading. I nodded for her to continue. She whispered she had a final request. She asked me to swear on the name of the Mountain King that I would see to its being fulfilled."

"What was it?" Seeing how unsettled Hilda was from the experience, I indicated the newly vacated chair.

Hilda shook her head, her face twisted, eyes staring blankly ahead.

"She asked that she be buried in the vault with her sister who died here recently."

An odd request, but why had this upset Hilda so greatly? "An easy enough petition to grant, I am sure. I will ask the head steward to see to it directly." Obeying an impulse, I gave Hilda a quick hug, though neither of us were naturally demonstrative. "Go rest, have some tea." I rang the bell lightly. "You have the name of the sister, I presume?"

Then came her words, a solemn tolling.

"Her sister's name was Grumwold."

~*~

That evening, I turned to the only recourse I had for misery: I took Adara out for a ride. I reeled in shock. For now, the crisp air and warmth of Adara's back kindled a sense of peace.

The news about Mesda had already spread. Everyone was horrified to discover that the sister of their revered lawmaker and head justice had died a lonely, impoverished servant. Both the head cook and laundry mistress were said to have bemoaned the hard work they had heaped upon the "intruder," and other servants hung their heads at their callous treatment of the old woman.

But none was as guilty as I was. I directed Adara to the Great River and slid off her back while she drank. The water cooled my dusty feet, a fast-flowing blessing cleansing a multitude of careless intentions and arrogant neglect. Had I but taken the time to talk with Mesda to understand her purpose in Marah. She could have fulfilled a very different role than that of laundress or potato peeler. And, of course, her final days would not have been ones of drudgery…nor perhaps have come so quickly. Drying my feet on the moss, I remounted my horse and shook away thoughts of Grumwold and my parents. It was good they were not here to see my failure. How important now more than ever that I proved myself capable of leadership. Perhaps I could expunge my guilt through success in battle. I turned my back on the Great River's healing current and rode home.

Anna and Hilda were waiting outside my chamber when I returned. Their faces betrayed anxiety.

Hilda ventured the first word. "My lady, perhaps, with your health, it was not advisable to take such an extended ride."

"We were getting to be worried sick," Anna piped in. "No, sit—we have tea here, and some nourishing broth. I will remove your boots myself, and I won't leave until every drop has been consumed."

Hilda took down my hair and brushed it carefully while I ate, murmuring words of comfort and encouragement. I gratefully sank into the calming routine.

"My lady," Anna stared at my feet.

"Anna?" I said, not in a hurry.

Anna threw up her hands. "Truly? Wet feet? As if it wasn't difficult enough to treat this confounded fever of yours." She waved dramatically at Hilda, nearly hitting a maid who had bustled in to collect the empty dishes. "She cannot ride around for a few minutes like a normal person. She must ride around for hours, while still sick, and must also soak her feet to catch her death of cold."

Hilda grunted behind me.

Anna rubbed my feet vigorously with a towel, whether to help or punish me. "We ought never to have let you go out. If only that nasty old wom—" Anna's mouth shut tight at a kick from Hilda.

"Do you want assistance preparing for bed, my lady?" Hilda asked. "Or shall we leave you for the night?"

I waved her away. "Go, rest. I thank you for your kind ministrations this evening, and I really am sorry I worried you." I squeezed Hilda's hand. "You showed kindness to more than just me today. Again, I thank you."

Hilda nodded, her eyes misty as she left the room.

I barely managed to change out of my riding clothes before collapsing on my bed.

"Couldn't the old hag have died with her secrets

and left us all without the added burden of knowledge and regret?" Anna whispered to a maid as they put out the lights.

But Anna hadn't intended for me to hear so I said nothing.

The next morning, I fulfilled the promise Hilda gave on my behalf, commanding that Mesda would receive a full, honorable funeral.

A few days later, I found myself heading the procession to the chapel. The procession reflected as in a mirror the one held not so long ago for this lady's honored sister. Both funerals were conducted with the ceremony proper for a respected person. A bird would have believed them the same. But how opposite the treatment of and regard for each woman had been while they were living. And I had been the one responsible for that treatment. My dark veil and dress hid a heart heavy with regret. Bless Hilda. She had completed a lion's share of the funeral preparations, had even insisted she take on the duties of the all-night vigil the evening before. The villagers lined the streets in silent respect. When all was finished, Mesda's body was laid to rest in Grumwold's tomb.

But all too quickly, my remorse converted to irritation.

Rumors of Mesda's constant speaking about the Mountain King had begun spreading among the servants and villagers. Somehow, the old woman had wielded influence even as she worked in the depths of the castle.

"Call for help from the Mountain King."

Her messages echoed, haunting me.

Servants, villagers, advisors, and even Hilda, hinted that perhaps asking for the help of the Mountain King wasn't such a bad idea after all. These hints, however, served merely to fuel the fire growing in my soul. I would prove myself capable without his help.

I embarked on what I'd decided was the best course of action after the scouts' frustrating news. But the following part of this history is hazy to me, and I cannot provide as much detail as I would wish. The fault is my own—I did not take the physicians' advice, and despite my poor health, I began a kingdom tour. Traveling in a retinue with Anna as my caretaker, I journeyed from village to village to offer encouragement and take stock of the kingdom's progress. Flags and laughter and good food made courageous appearances at every stop. But all was not well. Despite Anna's close watch, it was obvious that my health was wearing down again, and fast. Anna continued to blame Mesda for this physical decline. Almost nightly, as she settled onto her cot in our shared tent, she muttered, "Curse that bothersome servant woman. If she hadn't riled Lady Judah up with her secrets and messages, she wouldn't be out riding and marching about like a madwoman. Fussing herself to an early grave, I shouldn't wonder."

I was supposed to be asleep, so I let her be.

We camped within one more day's ride back to the castle, relieved to raise the colorful pavilions for the final time. Anna helped me prepare to rest before dinner.

"My lady, please take some of this wine before you nap." Anna continued to fluff pillows and lay out rugs, but my cup remained untasted. "My lady." Anna paused to examine my face. "You are pale. How do you feel?"

My attempt at smiling was unsuccessful. I picked up the cup and listlessly swirled the wine before putting it down. "Tired, Anna—tired, and dreadfully, dreadfully discouraged, truth be told."

"The armed units and fortifications were not at the levels you were hoping to see," Anna offered.

Raising my hand to rub my forehead, my finger caught the edge of the wineglass. It shattered on the ground, spraying shards like tiny swords, pouring out wine like blood. One shard flew up and nicked Anna's cheek, and real blood dripped, mingling with wine. I stared, aghast. Was this a prophetic sign?

How much blood —the blood of my people—would be spilt?

I slammed the table with my fist.

Anna jumped.

"It is disgraceful, Anna. We cannot do anything with these preparations. Where are the glory days of my parents when the army was mighty and filled with well-trained warriors? The workings of war must have been as second nature to the people in those days, but look at what it is in our time." My face burned, and the dragon of fever raised its ugly head. "We are no longer a nation of warriors, but a nation of farmers and peasants—of plate and pitchfork, not shield and blade." Bitter tears came, and there was no blessing in the flow.

Anna knelt and took my hands like a beggar. "My lady, do not work yourself up so. All will become as it should be. You will see." She flew to fetch medication from the box. As she administered another dose, a messenger came to the pavilion.

"If you please, a scout wishes an urgent audience with the governor," the messenger whispered to Anna.

Anna moved to my side, but I had overheard the message and was already nodding permission to see the scout. "Perhaps, my lady, the advisers…?" Anna suggested.

"Yes, bring them in to hear." I splashed cold water on my face to disguise the puffiness around my eyes and nose. Anna finished cleaning up the wine before the scout and advisors entered the tent.

The scout cleared her throat nervously before speaking. "My lady, esteemed people. I'm afraid I am not the bearer of positive news."

Everyone remained silent.

My heart sank.

"I have received word from several reliable sources, and I was able to personally confirm some of their statements. As we feared, the southern kingdoms continue to move forward in their plans. Even worse, they will begin to congregate within a shorter period than originally believed."

I rose at those words, swaying with dizziness. A burst of chatter almost drowned out my broken gasps. "I—we—they must not—" Grabbing my head, I collapsed to the ground. Shocked cries broke through the haze blurring my senses. Strong hands assisted Anna to lay me on the couch and cover me with blankets. Worried voices conferred together nearby.

"She's burning up," Anna whispered. "We must get help. We need something beyond what the doctors have been able to provide."

"Perhaps now she may be persuaded to send for the Enlightened One," one advisor murmured.

"Yes. Oh, yes—she must allow that now." Anna cried. "Judah, dear Judah, can you hear me? Can you understand me?" She waved a bottle of smelling salts under my nose.

I forced my eyes open.

"You collapsed, my lady. It is time to call for greater help," Anna said. "I beseech you—we all beseech you—to send for the Enlightened One now. A messenger could be off in five minutes."

The advisors nodded and added their verbal assent. "Please, please listen to us, my lady, before it is too late."

I shuddered and sighed. "I suppose it has finally come to that. Yes, yes, you are right. Send the messenger. I—I must sleep now, I think—" I lost all energy even to speak, and dropped my head to the pillow.

CHAPTER 9

I learned later how close I came to the leaving this world altogether. Anna, lover of drama, and Hilda, lover of storytelling, both entertained me eventually with detailed accounts of the days following my collapse.

After my being "dragged into the castle unconscious and on the brink of demise," per Hilda, the Enlightened One had been summoned. The Enlightened One did not have a home. He would say, *the world is my home,* if asked. Somehow, he always found those who sought him, and the messenger Anna had sent soon returned with the report that the Enlightened One was on his way.

Hilda had brought back the elderly physicians. Hilda told me later that she would watch by my bed as I slept, my shallow breathing shuddering the blankets. The fever seemed to grow by the hour, she said, and I only regained consciousness sporadically.

I was conscious but past caring what happened as Hilda and Anna talked with the physicians. I remember Hilda's hand trembling as she arranged a fresh, cool cloth on my forehead. "Isn't there anything you can do to stall the fever? The Enlightened One is expected almost any day, but…"

The husband took one of my hands in his wrinkled ones, which were surprisingly strong for the years they held. His voice was calming. "The fever has been strange from the beginning. We had hoped, that with time and rest—"

"—the fever might disappear entirely," his wife finished, adding her hands to ours, like spokes on a wheel. "But it has clung with a vicious tenacity we have never before seen."

"Isn't there," Hilda choked a whisper, "anything you can do?"

"We can make her more comfortable," the doctor said, stroking my forehead. "We are doing all in our power." He sighed. "I'm afraid greater skill is needed if she is to be saved."

"I had wanted to call for help from the Mountain King," Hilda said.

"Yes," he said. "Perhaps, if we even now send a messenger to the forest for the Mountain King—"

"No." Anna had slipped in and must have heard the last remark. "Hilda, you know Lady Judah wouldn't want that. And she already agreed to have the Enlightened One come."

"But where is he?" Hilda shot back. "You are so determined to have this Enlightened One come, and yet Lady Judah rests on what could be her deathbed."

"Give a few more days," Anna begged. "He will come. He should be here any day now." She grabbed the physicians' hands that still held mine. "Can't you at least keep her stable for a few more days?"

"Safely, possibly three days..." the husband

replied cautiously, and his wife added her assent.

"There." Anna clapped her hands. "Hilda, promise me you won't do anything for three more days."

I moaned and stirred, trying to communicate my agreement.

"Three days," Hilda replied grimly. "If no one has come by then, I will request the advisors call for the Mountain King's aid."

Wraithlike, the hours glided by. My dreams were frequent and troubled. Anna and Hilda told me later that they barely slept what with helping nurse me and dealing with the endless messengers inquiring about my health. I was also told later that one came from the Mountain King, saying his master was ready to help me if I wished. Anna politely, but firmly, declined the messenger's offer in the governor's name.

Finally, on that third day, the fever reached its apex. I've been told that I shifted that morning from flushed and restless to ashen and still. Anna and Hilda refused to leave my side.

Hilda relayed that she took initiative and spoke with the advisors, making sure they were ready to send a messenger on the morrow to the Mountain King if no aid had arrived by then.

In a rare moment that evening when I was conscious enough to hear and understand what was going on, Anna and Hilda conversed nearby, so I listened. "Why doesn't the Enlightened One come?" Anna whispered hoarsely. There was a splash of linens in water. "Surely, he would not arrive too late. He must know how urgent is our plea."

"Perhaps he is distracted by something else he deems equally urgent?" Hilda replied. "Or perhaps he is a slow traveler? Someone with so much wisdom must be quite aged by now, and he may only be delayed by the tediousness of the journey."

"That is true—you may be right. Only I would think that someone with such great age would be wise enough to ride a steed for a journey like this." Anna must have wrung the linen too fiercely, for water sloshed noisily onto the floor.

"Careful," Hilda groused. Anna's sharp retort started but froze on her lips as a messenger entered the room, squealing and stammering. "He's here. This very moment. The Enlightened One is," she paused to take a gasping breath, "in the castle."

Anna and Hilda both dropped their linens in the tub and sobbed. The elderly physician growled, "It's about time," but his wife shushed him.

I longed to see this man when he arrived, so I forced my eyelids to flutter open. I squinted, blinked, trying to adjust to the candlelight. At that moment, a beaming maid entered and announced, "The Enlightened One has come." She was followed by a tall man wrapped in a cloak, his face shielded by the hood. He strode across the room and bent to touch my pale face. As he straightened, he unclasped his cloak and whipped it from his massive shoulders.

Everyone gasped.

There, towering above us all in perfect form stood a man of immense beauty. He seemed bathed in light. His hair was golden and wavy, his eyes dark brown, almost black in their depths. In a deep, quiet voice that trembled the very floors, he said, "It is good that you sent for me. I have arrived in time, but there is not a minute to lose."

~*~

The following morning, I awoke from a gentle sleep, slowly recalling the medication the Enlightened One had given me the previous night, which had seemed to have an immediate effect. By the time Anna and Hilda returned to my room the next morning, they found me sitting up in bed, sipping broth, and talking quietly with the handsome man who had saved my life. I waved and beckoned them closer. Taking their hands, I said, "My friends, my beloved friends." I paused, my tears flowing. "How can I thank you enough for your love, your dedication? My deepest thanks to each of you. I have done nothing to merit such friendship," and by then we were all hugging and crying.

Gesturing for them to sit and join the conversation, I continued, "I believe you have already met Kiran."

He smiled at their obvious surprise.

I, too, had felt surprised. He actually had a normal name, not merely the mysterious title? Perhaps the seeming angel of light was human, after all. "We have just been discussing the final treatment, one that can dispel this fever forever."

Kiran—goodness, he was handsome. It was difficult to tear my gaze from his face.

"We were talking about a cure for Lady Judah's malady." Kiran picked up the dialogue.

"But I thought you cured her last night," Anna interrupted.

"That was a passing help, immediate relief to halt the fever's progress. But it works temporarily; the fever will return." Kiran cleared his throat. "There is but one method for ridding a person of this type of fever, an ancient method now known only to me. It is effective…but costly."

Anna jumped up. "We will do anything to pay for a treatment that will cure her."

"Not that kind of costly, dear Anna," I gently interposed. "He means I will have to make a difficult decision."

Hilda spilled the tea mid pour. "What sort of decision? Will there be a quest? I could go on a quest to help her."

I shook my head.

"This ancient method involves a type of…*substitution,* for a simple way of explaining it. The infected person can be freed from the malady by trading it for something else." He gazed at Anna and Hilda. "If Lady Judah wishes to be healed, she must decide what she is willing to trade: the sight in either her left or right eye, or the hearing in either her left or right ear."

The stunned silence was broken by a little cough from me. My eyes started to tear up, but I brushed away the drops before they could form. I straightened grimly. "You see, I have a difficult decision to make."

"You must be healed, no question about that," Anna cried, grabbing my hand as if by sheer force of will she could bring health.

Hilda dabbed her eyes and said nothing.

"Hilda?" I probed.

She blew her nose. "Perhaps..." She glanced at Kiran and then leaned close and whispered, "Perhaps the Mountain King...?"

I set my mouth and shook my head.

Hilda sighed. "Is there no other way?"

"None." Kiran reached out and touched her hand. She jumped at the contact. "You care deeply about your mistress. I can see that." He turned to me. "Do not, of course, make your decision lightly."

I laughed but wanted to weep. "I wish to jest that at least I have an eye or ear to spare—but I'm afraid I will too greatly miss the loss of any one of them." I leaned back, staring out the window.

Steady rain pooled outside. Slowly, a drop formed, and then fell. Drop...drop...drop...

After an eternity, I sat up, my decision firm. "My left ear's hearing. That is what I will surrender for the defeat of this fever."

"Are you sure, my lady?" Hilda's words trembled.

Anna cried.

I nodded slowly. "Sight would affect my ability to ride and fight, and I believe I use my right ear more frequently as it's on my dominant side..." My words trailed off. A few tears finally fled down my face.

Hilda took my hand and squeezed it.

I smiled at her and sat taller. "What must I do? Is it

painful?"

Kiran unexpectedly beamed. His deep voice was soothing and melodious, calming a sea of swirling emotions. "On the contrary, it is considered to be a very pleasant treatment—delicious, even." He turned to Anna and Hilda. "If one of you ladies will fill a cup with pure water…"

Anna sprang up and dashed out of the room. She brought a golden goblet fashioned like a lily, brimming with clear water. Kiran thanked her and took the goblet, placing it on a nearby table. He removed a handful of packets from the leather pouch hanging by his side.

We stared unblinking while Kiran poured the powders into the goblet and stirred, murmuring something unintelligible. Magically, the goblet he brought back was now filled with a rich, red liquid. This he handed to me with the instructions to drink all of it, slowly.

I took a nervous sip. "Why, it is wine, or perhaps just like wine." I laughed, gazing in wonder at the drink. "Truly, this is the most delightful liquid I have tasted in my life. Would that it were just a common drink, instead of the means of losing my..." I stopped.

Hilda looked at me sharply, but then I squared my shoulders, held the cup up to Kiran in a small toast, and drained the liquid. My facial muscles relaxed as I leaned back on my pillows. "I am—so tired—"

I could feel myself fading. Kiran watched me intently. "She will sleep deeply now for several hours while the treatment works. When she awakes, however—" he turned a little to smile at my friends "—she will be as good as new, I promise you."

CHAPTER 10

The rain must have continued through the night, for great puddles turned the gardens below into a series of small lakes. A pair of ducks was enjoying the situation immensely, and their morning chatter pulled me from deep sleep. I was about to ring for tea when someone pounded on my door. My heart dropped. Were we under attack?

"C—" I cleared my throat. "Come in."

A messenger almost fell into the room, her breath in hot gasps. As I flew from the window to her, Anna and Hilda tumbled in behind her, scolding like disgruntled hens.

"What is it?" I pulled over a chair and handed her a glass of water. "Please sit. Tell me what has happened."

Hilda and Anna gawked at us.

A sigh burst like steam came from the woman as she wiped water from her lips. I stared at her frozen, desiring to know the worst but still reveling in ignorant hope. "My lady, I rode hard from Naphtrona with this message." She pulled from her satchel a scroll, its seal intact. I snatched it, my hands shaking.

The seal cracked open, and Anna gasped.

The tension must have been too much for Hilda,

for she muttered something about collecting food for the messenger and left the room as I began reading.

I almost cried with relief.

Just as evil events seem to arrive together, so also do good things. Only two days after the arrival of the Enlightened One, here was news that a flood had struck the southern kingdoms, causing extensive damage and delaying their preparations for war.

In other words, we had been given the gift of time.

Hilda found the three of us hugging and crying when she brought in two plates of hot food. Anna squealed the joyful news, dragging Hilda into the happy fray. "You mean we haven't been overrun?" Hilda gasped, extracting herself. "I was so certain we were under attack that I almost brought my sword and shield with the plates."

The messenger, who was already devouring the contents of one, waved gratefully. "I brought a second for you, my lady, as you are looking so perky walking around already."

I laughed. "Is that why you two seemed so shocked when you came in? Because I was up and about?"

Anna and Hilda nodded. "It's like a miracle," Anna trilled, clapping her hands like a child. "The Enlightened One has healed you." We smiled together for a moment, and then they stared at me in an awkward fashion before glancing at each other.

"What?" I said, mystified.

Hilda nodded toward the messenger. "She was just talking to you," she whispered. "She's congratulating you on your recovery."

I startled. I had heard nothing. It was as if…*Ah, but I am. My left ear—I can no longer hear on that side.* I almost cried again right there—this time, not for joy—but I gritted my teeth and plastered on a smile before turning around. "I'm so sorry. Would you mind repeating that?

~*~

Although my people continued defense preparations, the urgency had abated and things settled temporarily. I was even able to enjoy my routines as before, walking in the garden, taking Adara out for rides, practicing with my bow, and managing the usual affairs of state.

I felt revived almost completely overnight, although it was difficult to adjust to hearing with only one ear. It took even longer for other people to remember my loss of hearing. It became such a problem that Anna and Hilda started to tease me about it, suggesting that a new court etiquette rule be issued in which no one was allowed to walk on the left side of the governor. I rolled my eyes, but my deficit brought an unexpected loneliness. The moon was no longer full; a half-moon glowed, and the rest lay in darkness. Had I ever thought about how much I treasured hearing? I discovered value through loss. I treasured what I no longer had.

Kiran, however, seemed at ease communicating with my limitation. He took great care to speak in my right ear. If standing on my left side, he situated himself so I could notice visual cues. This was such a relief that I sought his company more and more frequently. When I was with him, I felt comfortable and accepted. He was so wise, so understanding. Not to mention, of course, he was incredibly handsome. Goodness, how could one man have been gifted with such striking beauty?

Anna caught me mooning about this particular observation one day as I stood at an upper window overlooking the gardens. "My lady?" she asked.

I spun around.

In two steps, she was at my side, looking out the window.

Kiran stood below, leaning on a giant tree, gazing toward the valley.

"Ah." Her eyes twinkled mischievously. "I see you're enjoying the gorgeous view."

"The flowers are particularly beautiful this afternoon." My ears felt hot.

"Yes, yes, *so* beautiful. I suppose you really ought to head down for a stroll to appreciate them." She laughed.

I straightened my shoulders. "Actually, it just so happens that I already was on my way to do that very thing."

"Excellent."

"In fact, I was just about to give a tour of the gardens to Kiran. He asked if I would mind, since he and I are both so fond of gardens."

"Very fond."

"Unless you have some objection to my going for a stroll?" I raised my eyebrow.

"On the contrary," Anna winked, "I wish you all the best on your…stroll. I only must confess my jealousy should you succeed in your conquest, that is, your stroll."

From that time onward, long walks in the castle gardens with Kiran became a daily afternoon ritual.

During our walk one afternoon, I brought up the situation with the southern kingdoms and told Kiran about our defense preparations. "If you have any suggestions, I would be grateful to hear them." I hesitated. "This is my first time leading my people in war, and I understand you have more experience in this area." My face warmed a little. "I am determined to do this on my own, but I realize that some advice could prove useful."

Kiran's face turned grave. "Ah, my lady, that is a heavy burden you place on me. How is one to give sound advice to such a noble, fearless leader as you in such a brief time? They would need to spend considerable time in the situation, live among the people, before—"

"Then you should stay," I interrupted, impulsively grabbing his arm and throwing a pleading look as he turned. "You will stay, won't you?" I laughed. "You have me acting boldly in my eagerness for you to stay." *Heavens, Judah, since when did you become such a flirt?* But it was too late to change course. And besides, I rather liked holding his arm.

Kiran gazed at me. "I like it. Recklessness suits

you." He held my gaze a minute longer. "You almost have me convinced."

"What do I need to do to convince you completely?"

"Keep holding my arm like that."

I flushed. But Kiran winked and laughed so winningly that I pretended to be completely put out, smacking his arm lightly with my fan for his impertinence. However, I left my hand where it was, and we continued walking.

Kiran accepted my invitation to remain and assist with the war crisis. He also requested permission to allow his own retinue to join him. "All are men of great knowledge, skillful warriors as well as gentlemen," he assured me. They arrived soon after.

And such a company. When the gates opened amid cheerful trumpet blasts, I believe all jaws dropped. Every single man—about thirty of them—was tall, graceful, strong, and almost unbelievably handsome. Level noses, firm lips, square chins, bright eyes looking out from under luxurious heads of straight hair, curly hair, beards and moustaches and clean-shaven faces, beautifully cut garments of tasteful colors and styles—the variety was stunning. I was told that even the village men admitted the company cut dashing figures as they marched to the castle doors. Women crowding the castle windows shrieked with delight. I watched the procession from my room along with my attendants. Anna was rendered useless as she exploded into giddy spasms. Hilda, who seemed to be the only one unimpressed with the guests, had to shake Anna to remind her to finish preparing for the reception.

Every man was introduced to me in the great hall. I was amused to hear later that some of the courtiers had commented to Hilda that it was difficult to tell who was more gracious—the poised governor extending hand to each new guest or the debonair men with sweeping bows and murmured gratitude. It was obvious how Anna's admiration grew with each man who passed before her. To be fair, even my eyes were turned somewhat in that display of masculine glory. The very last man offered a particularly deep bow. "My lady," he murmured, "we are most grateful for your courteous hospitality."

"You are all quite welcome, I can assure you," I replied with a smile. "I believe everyone in the castle will be very happy to make your further acquaintance."

"Likewise, I look forward to making theirs. We are almost overwhelmed to see so much talent and beauty in one place." This man must have noticed Anna, who was gazing at his striking face and wavy red hair, because he gave her the faintest wink as he stood from his bow to rejoin his group.

"A real charmer," Hilda observed under her breath to no one in particular. I nearly snorted as she rolled her eyes over Anna's dreamy sighs, which inevitably would peak in wild gushing late into the night.

After the initial flurry, Kiran's retinue became familiar elements in the castle routine. In fact, it was hard to remember what life had been like before their arrival. They went on hunting trips and arranged countless celebrations, parties, and theatricals for courtiers and villagers alike. They played instruments, sang, and flirted with maids and attendants and courtiers. They painted, ate, and played games with great abandon and enjoyment. Hardly an unattached young woman remained who had not loudly lost her heart to at least one of the young men. Hilda complained about Anna's shameless, continual flirtation with the redheaded gentleman and neglecting of her duties, but I think she was more piqued about taking her evening walks alone.

Although my concentration was with matters of state, even I had started to notice Anna's new attachment. I took tea on my balcony one morning while the pair meandered through the gardens below. Anna's vivacious laughter at her companion's teasing floated up to my balcony. I sipped, mused, listened. This was becoming quite serious. Perhaps it was time to say something to Kiran about this flirtation since Anna was under my protection. I wandered into my rooms, absently fingering one of the curtains fluttering in the breeze. I'd bring it up today. Kiran would surely know about his friend's intentions.

That afternoon, I made sure Anna was busy in the castle before setting off with Kiran on our regular walk. I steered him from our usual route to settle cozily on a bench.

"But what is this? More recklessness?" he joked after ensuring I was comfortable.

Kiran did bring out a spark of unruliness in me that I had not known before, and I rather liked it. I've always known pride and vanity to be my vices. But up until now, no one could have accused me of being too much fun.

I wanted to rest my hand on his arm. I suspected he would have welcomed it. But I fought off the urge to flirt. This was serious business. Instead, I waved my hand. "How dare I be so bold as to deviate from routine? O Enlightened One, surely you already knew that I brought you here to interrogate you."

He laughed, and I laughed. Now for the serious part.

"I wonder, Kiran, about your redheaded young man—what is his name again? I'm certain you've noticed that he seems to be stealing the heart of one of my favorite attendants. Her parents both died years ago, and I am responsible for her as well as quite fond of her. What is he like? Are his intentions worthy of someone who I also consider a friend? If I am to be left quite desolate, then he had better be worthy."

Kiran laughed. "She has excellent taste. Broden is one of my very best, and she would be lucky to catch him. His intentions are honorable, of course." Kiran stood and pulled out a small knife such as was used for cutting flowers. "But why worry about losing one attendant? You ought to have many more, you know, than you can fit here in this sweet little castle."

"What do you mean?" I giggled over the flower Kiran offered me from a nearby bush and tried to weave it into my thick hair, which I had begun to wear loose and flowing in the afternoons. "What are you talking about? Why would I possibly need more attendants?"

"Why, royalty ought to have a full entourage available at beck and call, you know."

I froze. Why did he look so serious? "Kiran. What are you saying?"

"You mean you don't know?"

"Know what?" The hairs on the back of my neck tingled.

"Know that your parents were only posing as governors, and you are really the daughter of a king and queen? Royal blood flowed through their veins." Kiran's eyes twinkled as I blanched. "Lady Judah, didn't you know that you are a princess, and as such," he took my hand gently and bowed to kiss it, "you are heir to the throne of this kingdom?"

~*~

Kiran seemed to be holding a vial of smelling salts to my nose. My head finally stopped spinning, but I lay still and focused on breathing. Why was I on the ground? What just happened? A single word, *royalty,* rose in my mind.

A princess?

Eventually, queen?

How was that possible? Why had my parents never told me? Grumwold surely knew. Why didn't she tell me after they died? All these years—not only a governor, but also a princess. I'd always assumed my betrothal to royalty was the Mountain King rewarding two governors who had served him well. Not because I was, myself, royalty.

I attempted to sit up.

Kiran kneeled nearby and watched my face.

"How do you know these things?" I whispered.

"I know many things," he replied, his voice quiet. "It is my way." He helped me to the bench.

I groaned and held my head. "Why did my parents not tell me of this?"

"Perhaps they felt a deception was harmless. And they may have felt it was…safer…for you to assume a royal title through marriage." His voice dropped lower. "I am sure they never wished to harm your chance of proving yourself a valiant queen by your own merit, able and capable of regaining her rightful title and throne."

A messenger's sudden appearance interrupted Kiran. "I am at your disposal, my lady, if you wish it," Kiran whispered into my good ear.

I still felt dazed, but I tore my eyes from Kiran's face and managed a short nod to the newcomer.

"Two riders approach the castle, my lady. They will arrive in a few minutes." The messenger spoke too loudly, awkwardly overcompensating for my deaf ear.

I raised my eyebrow, but smiled. "Thank you. Pray, where are the riders from? What are their colors?"

"Blue and white, my lady. They come from the palace of the Mountain King."

CHAPTER 11

It was as though I, a fish, had been shown hidden wings. What limits were there for me but the heavens with wings such as these?

Hilda has always been observant. She raised an inquiring eyebrow as she helped me settle into my chair in the great hall. She flushed, moved to my right ear, and whispered again, "What is it?"

"Later," I murmured.

Trumpets announced the messengers from the Mountain King, and all rose in respect. To my astonishment, instead of the usual lord or lady serving as ambassador, a woman who appeared about my age walked in boldly, followed by a servant bearing a gold box. The woman was stunning, almost radiant, but not with traits regularly associated with great beauty. Rather, her eyes were electrifying. She was dressed entirely in white, and her hair, thick and straight and midnight black, was parted down the middle and hung past her waist. She strode to the dais where I waited.

Was she coming all the way up?

At the last moment, I stepped out and met her at the bottom of the dais.

We bent low in greeting to each other.

"Greetings, highly favored one." Her words broke

the silence like a clap of thunder.

What a strange greeting. Who could this be?

"The son of the Mountain King sends the Lady Judah gifts as a proclamation of the day when he shall himself be with you."

My heart raced. Two shocks in one day. "He is coming? The son of the Mountain King? When?"

"The son of the Mountain King will come to you when the time is right," the lady replied.

"You are not authorized to tell me the exact time?"

"I am but a servant of the Mountain King and of my lady. I have spoken what I was commanded to say." She smiled, kindness enrobed in the formality. She raised her hand, and the servant held up the gold box. "The first gift"—the box opened, and I gasped—"a star diamond, which at its heart bears the shape and radiance of a star. There is none like it in the world. It is intended to be worn as a daily ornament, reminding its wearer of the gift-giver's imminent arrival." The lady held out the gorgeous jewel on a delicate gold chain, and it shone with white fire. Its setting, although simple, was of beautiful workmanship. "May I?"

I nodded, speechless, and leaned forward for the lady to fasten the diamond around my neck.

"For his second gift, the son of the Mountain King sends my lady a voice."

Another strange gift? "A…where is it?"

"Here, my lady." The woman spread out her hands. "I am the voice, the last gift. I proclaim the coming of the son of the Mountain King."

I gaped. I sputtered. I did everything a lady in my

position knew not to do in a formal exchange. Not another Mesda. Please, not again. "You? What am I to do with you?"

The lady waited, and I blushed at the gracelessness of my words. "I am honored by the gifts. I am honored by your presence here. What role are you to have? What does a *voice* do?"

The lady bowed her head. "I am my lady's humble servant. I will serve my lady."

Uncertain what to say, I chose a simple, "Thank you." Then I added in a low voice, "Am I understanding correctly that you are sent here in the capacity of a…a servant? With the intention to work here as such?"

For the second time, the woman smiled. "Yes, my lady, to begin immediately in the way that suits you."

"Pray, what is your name?"

"They call me Raven, my lady."

"Raven."

Kiran's words flashed through my mind. Here was an opportunity to have three attendants instead of merely two. "I am pleased to have you join me as a personal attendant, Raven. Hilda and Anna will show you to your quarters. When you have eaten and rested, they will familiarize you with the way of things here." I signaled behind me.

For the first time ever, Hilda missed her cue, and I turned to see what had happened. Anna was not in attendance, but I had a guess about where she was and who she was with.

I coughed, and Hilda snapped up her head. Our

eyes met. Was she wondering about Anna's absence? No, that wasn't it. She was looking at me curiously, her eyebrow raised. I'd known Hilda long enough to practically read the thoughts in her eyes. *Another attendant? Since when did Lady Judah wish for a third attendant?* But there was no time for her to react or protest. Hilda nodded, and turned to lead her new co-attendant out of the hall.

"Oh, Raven." I had just remembered something, my voice rising with a friendly laugh.

Raven paused.

"The letter... You have forgotten the letter from the son of the Mountain King."

Raven peered at me. "There is no letter, my lady."

"No…letter?" My expression took longer to control this time. "No letter? Are you quite sure?"

"I am certain, my lady."

"Perhaps the letter was forgotten at the palace—"

"I received my directions and your gift from the Mountain King himself, my lady. There is no letter."

I had to regain command of myself. I had just discovered I was a princess, after all, and must behave as such. But what did this mean? There was always a letter. "Thank you. That will be all." My cheeks grew warm, and I pretended to not notice the whispering around the room as I walked out. No letter.

Finally, in the safety of my private sitting room, I dropped onto the couch and burst into tears. Perhaps my betrothed had forgotten about me. But then, why would he have sent a star and a voice, strange gifts though they were? I stood. I paced. I paused for a critical look in the mirror. Perhaps he changed his mind. Perhaps he no longer loved me or wanted me. Could it be that these gifts were actually parting gifts? I sniffed. "It's not like I know him, after all. I don't need him." But his letters—I felt like I knew his heart through the letters, and through his beautiful gifts. "I'm sure it's nothing. I'm just silly." I viciously kicked a stray pillow. The pillow knocked over a small table, shattering a vase of flowers over the floor. *Unless I'm not.*

My inner war continued until Hilda's and Raven's voices floated under the door. I grabbed a shawl and fled down the back stairs into the twilight.

"Why the troubled face, my lady? I hope your visitors have not brought ill news?"

I jumped when Kiran found me in the gardens but smiled when his face came into view. "No—only some things are rather confusing. I suppose you never feel confused, do you?" I tried to subtly rearrange my disheveled hair, but I feared the worst. I hoped my eyes weren't puffy.

Kiran laughed. "Not frequently."

"A lot has happened in the last few hours. I would like to sort it all out."

Kiran joined me on the bench. "I'm sure at least some of this has to do with the subject I brought up when we spoke earlier." When I didn't reply, he, too, fell silent, and together we watched the last glows of light fade.

As darkness closed over the land, lamps were lit in the rooms behind us. Our shadows, side by side, stretched out toward the horizon. I knew what I needed to do. "Kiran, I am meeting with my advisors in our war council room this evening. Will you come and share what you have shared with me?"

Kiran bowed. "I will come."

~*~

That night during the war council, the usual ideas were proposed and discussed and rejected. The usual gnashing of teeth at the slow progress, inefficient training, and insufficient resources predictably overwhelmed us. Throughout it all, Kiran sat listening, observing. Finally, one of the oldest advisors called on him. "You have not yet voiced your thoughts, O Enlightened One. Perhaps you have ideas you would share with us?"

"With your permission, my lady?" Kiran met my gaze as if seeking approval.

I hesitated and then nodded. This had better be the right decision. It would be impossible to go back. I hid my quivering hands under the table.

"My lords and ladies, esteemed advisors, today I have given information to your governor that affects you almost as much as it does her. This information relates to the facts surrounding her birth…" Kiran proceeded to explain that I was, by right of birth, a princess, and, therefore, heir to the throne of the kingdom, a future queen. "And as such, I counsel that we desist from our habits of hesitation. I advise that our future queen act boldly to prove herself a leader by royal right and regain her due status." Kiran turned to me. "The people, such as they are, will stand behind you, Lady Judah, and you will inspire them to even greater deeds once the time is right to make the facts of your birth known abroad." Kiran's voice became even more solemn. "This kingdom must conquer the enemies who dare to threaten its borders and its freedom. To guarantee the success of this most sacred of quests in the face of such desperate odds, it is possible that the need for aid from an ally is at hand." His gaze darted around the room. "However, I may have ways of assisting you in this, as well."

All eyes bored into him.

Kiran waved his hand. "But the time is not yet right for details. Some things must happen first. Please, continue your conversation."

"Lord Kiran, what is the difference between a princess and a queen? Or what must a princess do to become a queen?" Everyone froze at this final question the youngest council member put to Kiran.

Kiran's reply was brief. "According to the law of the land? Marriage. A princess must be married to become a queen." His eyes met mine. "But she may choose her own husband."

CHAPTER 12

I held the scarf—soft, long, blood red—to my dark curls longer than necessary, approving the effect in the mirror. Kiran would like this. A light knock interrupted my daydreaming. "Who is it?"

"My lady?" The voice was muffled by the door. "Would you like help dressing now?"

"Oh, yes, of course—come in, ladies." Laughing, I held up the scarf. "As you can see, I've already started without you. But where is Anna?"

Hilda sniffed and rolled her eyes.

"She was engaged in the garden this morning, my lady, and we decided to not to disturb her," Raven responded kindly.

"Really? I am surprised. The morning dressing selection was always Anna's favorite routine. Ah, well. Raven—" I beamed at her "—I want you to know how impressed I've been. You have taken to the role with speed, skill, and talent."

"She is good at everything, my lady." Hilda put a dress back as I indicated riding clothes were needed and presented three others appropriate for activity. "With Anna being so, ahem, busy all the time now, I've given many of her previous tasks to Raven." She laid the dresses on the bed. "Raven seems to have a sixth sense for what is needed without being told, and I often find my own tasks completed before I've started. She's going to give me bad habits if I'm not careful." Hilda laughed.

"I see." I held up each garment in turn. "The gray one, I think, with the red scarf for color. Do you get along well with Anna?" This last question I directed to Raven.

Hilda coughed. "I think, my lady, that the more accurate question is, does Anna get along with Raven?"

"Peace, friend." Raven smiled. "It is difficult when someone unfamiliar disrupts waters of routine. It will take time for the flow to find new rhythms."

"Speaking of adjusting—" I held up the scarf again, "Raven, dear, do you think you could wrap my hair up in that lovely style you did the other day? I plan to ride Adara this morning, and I would like to keep these curls back somehow."

~*~

I really was pleased with Raven, and I was still more pleased when Hilda and Raven established a firm friendship. Outside of Anna and myself, Hilda had never had many close friends, preferring a few confidantes over many acquaintances. Now that Anna was distracted by the redheaded young man, I was glad to see another friend enter Hilda's life. However, I suspected Anna was offended when many of her favorite tasks were reassigned to the person she disparagingly called the "new girl." She'd taken an intense disliking to Raven.

Raven never seemed to notice Anna's snubs and irritated looks, but Hilda's sharp remarks to Anna attested that she noted every bit of Anna's rude behavior. Hilda could be found either with Anna or with Raven, but seldom with both in the same room.

Anna herself seemed to avoid Raven's company whenever possible.

I felt mildly annoyed by the tension between my attendants, but generally ignored it. However, before long it became apparent that Raven was causing ripples beyond the bounds of my close circle. How could this be? She hardly spoke until she was spoken to, and it seemed impossible to offend her. But the other servants held Raven in a sort of awe.

Granted, her appearance made her stand apart. She dressed simply in all white, which contrasted sharply with her long black hair. Her demeanor was that of a confident, independent woman. Although she was friendly and kind to all, she held herself aloof and did not "fit in," as the cook put it to Hilda.

Raven seemed to choose to be alone for stretches of time when she had breaks, going for long walks out in the fields and forests. That lonely habit soon waned for those in Marah had discovered they could hear beautiful tales of the palace of the Mountain King from her. It was noted how small crowds often gathered when Raven sat with a cup of tea or walked along the cobbled streets. Perhaps her popularity irritated Anna even more. Hilda mentioned she had quite the time of it trying to keep Anna from picking petty battles with her perceived competition.

Anna was not the only castle inhabitant at odds with Raven. The ever-informed Hilda told me that the young men in Kiran's retinue each tried, in turn, to lure Raven's attention, bringing compliments and flowers and invitations to dances. However, she quietly resisted all of them. What surprised me even more was to hear that when they finally understood Raven would have nothing to do with them, they began to bring a different kind of offering: insults and mockery and tricks, but when these also failed to spark a reaction from her, they left her, by and large, alone.

By then I had seen firsthand the excessive badgering. I brought it up one day when Raven joined me in the garden. "I see the young men are finally giving you some space."

"Yes," she replied. A small smile played about her lips, but she offered nothing else.

What could she be thinking? Would she report this to the Mountain King? "I hope they were not too tiresome to you? Young men can sometimes push things further than they ought to without realizing they're being annoying," I pressed.

Raven handed a freshly clipped rose to me, but otherwise did not respond. She quietly continued trimming the bush.

I sighed. "Well, I hope you are enjoying living here at Marah, at least, although I imagine it must feel tedious after residing in the grand Mountain King's Palace."

At the mention of the palace, Raven straightened, and her countenance seemed to glow. She was just opening her mouth to speak when Kiran strode around the corner.

He glanced up and waved, his usual smile for me mixed with a flash of irritation at the sight of Raven.

"Ah, there you are." Kiran bowed over my hand and cleared his throat pointedly. "I'm afraid I must intrude for a few minutes. Privately, of course."

Raven stooped to pick up the basket of roses, and when she stood again, she seemed strangely tall next to Kiran. She peered gravely in his face for a second and then turned to me and bent her head. "My lady." She left as Kiran offered me his arm.

"You don't like Raven," I said as I took his arm.

He laughed. "She seems rather stuffy, don't you think? I wonder why she's here, anyway," he added, almost as an afterthought. "

"Well, you were just commenting the other day how someone of royal blood ought to have more attendants, so—now I have three."

My teasing brought a chuckle from Kiran.

"But you didn't come to talk about Raven, I think. That is, you were looking for me, I hope." I blushed.

"Nothing gets by you," Kiran said. "Yes, I'll admit that I was looking for you." He settled next to me on an obliging garden bench. "I have come to offer my services to you."

"But you already have." I playfully tapped his arm and laughed but stopped when I saw his face. "Kiran. What is it? Has something happened?"

"Something just might happen," Kiran drawled. "I am leaving for a time to go on a journey around this kingdom and beyond." A hint of a smile flickered on the side of Kiran's mouth. "I implied several days ago at the war council that I may have means of assisting you in this rising conflict. Unless your ladyship expressly forbids it," he mocked in a teasing manner. "I will go make arrangements to help you. These arrangements should enable you to establish yourself as the mighty ruler that you are, to show the world that you are worthy of your royal blood." His eyes sparked with fire. "And who knows—they may even prove the means of peace."

"If what you say proves to be so…" I struggled to collect my emotions. "How can I ever thank you?"

To my astonishment, Kiran took my hands into his own and pressed them. My heart fluttered strangely. My cheeks grew warm.

"Say that you will miss me?" His voice was soft.

"Why—yes—of course," I stuttered, my cheeks burning. What was wrong with me? I was acting like a schoolgirl. *Get ahold of yourself, Judah.* "I…I…I mean—when will you return?"

"I cannot say. Perhaps a few weeks. Perhaps longer." Then Kiran slowly, gently, kissed my hand. The spot where his lips touched seemed to burn.

I turned away, flushing anew, this time with enjoyment. Kiran reached for my averted face and softly turned my chin toward him. Wordless, he searched my eyes as if for the answer to a question. I know my eyes had to have glowed. When Kiran leaned over again, I was ready, and raised my lips to meet his.

Fire flowed through my veins.

Our embrace, although lingering, was over too soon. Kiran lightly traced the line of my chin, sighed, and abruptly stood. "I will leave most of my men to protect you, of course, but a few will be useful to me on my journey. Command the rest as you will." He smiled. "My lady," and then he bowed and was gone.

I sat in the garden, staring off in the direction where Kiran had left. Moments later, hooves clattered down the streets and out the gates. I followed them in my mind. I longed to rush up the stairs and watch Kiran from the wall.

Someone touched my elbow, and I jumped.

Hilda yelped.

"I'm so sorry, my lady." Hilda gathered the dropped towel and pieces of a small washing bowl that had taken flight. She flushed red.

"It's all right, Hilda. I'm sorry. Had you called me, too?"

"Only once or so."

If only I were still whole. I snapped a section of the broken bowl in half, scratching my finger in the process. Served me right for acting in frustration. Like a child, I stuck my finger in my mouth for a minute to stop the blood. "This is tedious, not hearing in that ear. Well, at least I'm alive."

Hilda gave me a quick hug. "And for that, we are all grateful," she said, hooking my arm with her own. "Now, my lady, it is time for tea, and I really insist that you come." She led me to a tea cart in the sunroom.

She poured a cup and arranged a plate of cake and fruit, glancing sideways at me all the meanwhile.

"Hilda, do you know that Kiran has left for a time?" I blurted, embarrassment warming my cheeks. The cup I held lurched dangerously. Only Hilda's nimble reaction as she caught my hand protected me from a scorching spill.

"Yes, my lady. Anna informed me of it before they departed." Hilda submerged her hand, which had suffered the burn I should have received, into a convenient bowl of floating lilies. She waved off my cries of concern with a flippant comment. "It seems her young fellow was one of the men he chose to take along," she continued. "However, I do not know the intent of their journey."

Absently, I stirred my tea. *Should I tell her about what happened in the garden?* I stared out the window as if expecting the answer to hang growing among the trees. Why not? "Hilda, before leaving, he—"

A servant entered with a flourishing bow and a message. "My lady, the shepherds have arrived. They request an audience."

I leaped up. The servant dodged as the rest of my tea flew through the air. "Shepherds? Here? Now?" I waved an apology and set down the cup.

The servant nodded solemnly, but a smile bloomed on his face.

Hilda's eyes were as wide and shining as I guessed my own to be, and I impulsively squeezed her hands. Would this day of wonders never cease? If only my parents and Grumwold could be here for this moment.

Sheep—it had been since before I was born that these miracles lived here. Without a ready supply of wool, any fabric finer and softer than what could be made with goats' hair had to be imported from outside the country and at great cost. And shepherds. Often had I heard tales of the peaceful influence their presence gave in the land before the Destruction. What great treasure came to my kingdom with the return of shepherds and sheep?

I peppered the servant with questions while rushing after him, but he only repeated that the shepherds were on their way to the great hall, and there were several of them. Hilda and I almost collided with Anna and her flyaway hair as she careened around the corner. Raven was absent for her time off, and that meant Anna would remain in a good mood.

"I just heard." Anna gasped. "Imagine. Real, live shepherds. I can hardly believe it." She hopped on alternating feet, clapping her hands. All three of us giggled in excitement as we flew to the hall. Two minutes' pause for deep breathing, and we had calmed down enough to enter the great hall with befitting dignity. A larger crowd than usual of courtiers, servants, and villagers gathered in the hall to see the shepherds. Real, live shepherds. People herded into tighter groups in order to fit everyone inside. For the first time in ages, the great hall was completely filled.

I settled into my seat, breathless, just as trumpets announced the guests' arrival. As one body, everyone rose, necks straining, eyes sparkling.

The great doors swung open, and seven ruddy

men strode in, all dressed in leathers and sheepskins. Their weathered faces were tanned and bearded, their hair, shaggy and wild. Their feet were shod in strong, flexible shoes, and each man bore great bundles on his shoulders. The men smiled. The smell of mountains and animals and sweat entered the room with their bright eyes. They walked up to the dais and, as if one man, they flung their bundles to the ground and stood up straight.

One man moved. He was short and stocky, his features homely. He did not act as one who enjoyed the limelight. Nevertheless, authority radiated from his person. He was obviously the leader. As he stepped forward, his voice rang out like a bell.

"Greetings and peace to you, Lady Judah."

CHAPTER 13

I stared at the shepherd. The court was frozen, silent, but as a frozen river is silent, whose waters thrum beneath with perpetual life. My heart throbbed, oddly warmed and quickened. Did others feel the same as I did, trying to understand what about him made the heart thrill? *Strange. He is rather plain, after all. His eyes, perhaps?* Yes, it must be his eyes—never had I seen eyes so piercing and fathomless. They seemed to see my very core self. A glad smile broke on my face as I stepped forward. "Greetings, honored shepherds—the kingdom has long missed your presence. Your appearance here this day is most welcome."

The man was also smiling warmly. "We have long desired to come, and the time is right." He swept the span of his companions with his arm, and his movements were free, easy. "We bear gifts for the Lady Judah and her household—simple gifts, which we hope you will accept." As one, the men unsheathed their long knives and cut the cords binding the bundles, unleashing avalanches of…snow? No, not snow—*wool,* wool as fine as the mysterious stash of wool Grumwold used for knitting years ago. Gasps tore around the court, puffy bales springing in the air when the cords released them—this was more wool than I am sure anyone here had seen in their lifetime. Snow-white wool, midnight-black wool, and earth-brown wool, all beautifully cleaned and carded. If only I could throw myself into the enchanting, swirling eddy.

I approached the closest pile as if in a trance, my hand extended to touch the cloud. Kneeling, I caressed the fibers between my fingers. I sensed every pair of eyes in the room following my actions, perhaps imagining the fibers between their own fingers. Did the joy that glowed within radiate on my face? Grumwold's supply would have paled alongside this mountain. I brushed away a few tears glimmering in the corners of my eyes. If only Grumwold could be here now. I abruptly stood up. "I—we—thank you, shepherds," I said. "I have never seen anything so beautiful in my life, I think."

The shepherds bowed, pleasure evident on their bronzed faces. Across the hall, people pressed forward. What a treasure to have piled on our own castle's floor.

The head shepherd—the man who had spoken earlier—cleared his throat. His eyes twinkled at me. Only then did I notice another bundle strapped to his chest, one that he now gently cradled while untying strong cords. "I have one more gift, my lady," he said, unfolding the leather wrapping and extending it to me.

Tears now sprang freely from my eyes, and I gasped "Oh," as the man lay the gift into my outstretched arms. Again, time froze. Through a haze rose his words: *orphan* and *ewe* and *yours*.

I am certain my face shone like a sunrise as I

snuggled the sweet bundle against my chest. There, for the first time since the shepherds left the land so long ago, lay a tiny, white lamb, tame and sleeping contentedly. The court swayed in stunned silence. Then thunderous applause and wild cheers erupted. A lamb. To stay, to live in Marah. The noise, of course, woke the sweet pet, which cried out in the loud, bleating voice that only little lambs own. The sound, everyone agreed, was the most beautiful of music.

"She is…incredible…" my whisper trailed off. I handed the lamb carefully to Anna, who had maneuvered to the best position and seemed only too thrilled to hold the adorable creature. But a cloak of caution now shrouded my unbridled joy. My parents had taught me a crucial principle: nothing comes free—everything has a cost.

I held out my hand to the head shepherd with a reserved smile. "How can I ever repay you…?"

"Abel. Please call me Abel." The man pressed my hand briefly and appeared as if he would laugh. At me? Surely not.

"How can I ever repay you, Abel, for these marvelous gifts?" I straightened to my full height. "What is it that you would request of me?"

Abel leaned in and tilted his head. "We would like to graze our flocks for the next few months in the narrow valleys and forests that lay east of the castle," he replied, watching me. The hint of a smile flashing on the edges of his mouth belied the gravity of the moment.

My jaw dropped. "But…but that is not a costly

request," I sputtered. "What is it you desire? What do you need?" I waved my hand at the piles of wool and at the lamb. "What do you truly hope to receive in exchange?"

"Only what I have said," Abel replied gently.

"There is hardly a real element of exchange if we are to benefit directly on both sides."

"But these are gifts," Abel smiled. "There can be no exchange." Again, those penetrating eyes. "Will you do us the honor, Lady Judah, of inviting us to those lands for a time?"

The crowd murmured, the excitement palpable. I stared, flabbergasted at their generosity. It was all I could do to not clap my hands in pleasure. It seemed the shepherds really were as generous and wonderful as in the tales. And they would stay. *Here.* I scooped the lamb from Anna's arms. "We are the ones who would be honored," I declared to shouts of approval from the crowd. "Please stay as long as you are able, and choose your place from the best in the land."

The shepherds bowed their heads and turned to leave. The crowd parted as the men strode forward and closed behind them.

Then all eyes returned to me.

"Beloved people," I said, "this is a blessed day, indeed." The crowd cheered as I smiled and began weaving my way through the people, holding the lamb for each person to touch.

Later, all three attendants joined me in my chambers to play with the lamb and marvel at its curly, sleek coat, perky ears, and tiny, pink tongue and nose.

Raven had been out walking in the western forest during this time, and she had missed seeing the shepherds. Now even Anna put aside her grudge to tell Raven of that exciting afternoon, how the shepherds had come and given their gifts. "But what an ugly man the head shepherd is." Anna giggled, gesturing with her hands to exaggerate the size of his nose and his wild hair.

I laughed. "Yes—his nose and mouth are quite large, and I'm afraid he hasn't had a proper haircut or beard trim in the last decade or so." Anna snorted. "Still," I mused, "he did have rather surprising eyes. It must be hard to be a plain person."

"You will never know, my lady," Hilda noted. "Even when you eventually age, you will always be a stunning beauty like your mother." She caught the pillow I threw at her and tossed it back, narrowly missing the tiny lamb snuggled on a nest of soft blankets.

"I wasn't fishing for compliments, but thank you." I turned back to my new pet, whom I'd shielded from Hilda's wild throw. "I shall call you Jemimah, my little dove," I cooed.

"A good name, my lady," Raven smiled. "They will make a shepherdess of you yet."

The attendants fussed over the lamb for a few more minutes, only stopping when a servant called for attention to other duties.

"Hilda, a moment, please," I whispered.

She paused and quickly returned.

"My lady?"

"I am going to visit the shepherds tomorrow—it's impossible to shake the idea growing in my mind."

"I am going with you," she asserted.

"I was sure you would." I clapped my hands and then leaned in, glancing around. "I would like an early start, and I would prefer that our destination…be kept secret."

"I will meet you at the stables a little before dawn, my lady, and we can inform the stableman about the direction we will head."

I squeezed her hand, and she left. It would be next to impossible to keep the spark of adventure out of my eyes, so for the rest of the evening I did my best to avoid the others completely.

~*~

By dawn we were riding out of the gates.

I had asked Raven to take care of Jemimah as I expected to be absent until evening. I did not elaborate, and Raven did not press for details. Even the groom only nodded when informed of our riding direction and asked if I would like any messages to be passed along before I left. Each detail fell smoothly into place. A promising start to our small adventure. Perhaps this bade well for the day. Perhaps we would fulfill our quest with ease.

Of course, neither Hilda nor I knew the exact location of the shepherds. The first streaks of sunlight touched the treetops as I led the way to the small valleys watered by mountain-fed brooks, the same ones I had explored as a child with my father. These would be ideal for flocks, and as we rode, I said I'd always dreamed of the day when the shepherds would return from afar to stay, perhaps for always.

We flew toward the forests, driven by hope and elation. Adara had not been taken out frequently since my accident, and she galloped as a golden streak across the wide valley and along the river that led to the forests. Hilda's mare had to work hard to keep up, but eventually both horses slowed to follow the forested paths overhung with low branches.

We broke out of the woods a few hours later. There lay the first of the narrow valleys, which was now lit brightly by the sun. A brook's song joined a glorious, unfamiliar sound: the cries of innumerable sheep scattered among hills and boulders. Shepherds moved among the flocks, some working, some watching, some singing or playing flutes in harmony with the stream. One man turned toward us as we rode out, and a great smile spread on his face. As he strode toward us, I recognized him as the head shepherd himself.

"Lady Judah," he called out. "Greetings, and welcome. And greetings to her ladyship's friend."

"Thank you." I had rehearsed this next part with Hilda on the ride over. I'd confessed to feeling embarrassed for following my impulse to seek out the shepherds. "I thought I ought to come and, well, learn how to best care for my little Jemimah, the new lamb you brought me." I flushed. Hilda tried to hide a smile—my discomfort must have kindled a desire to laugh.

"A good name." Abel had reached the horses by now, who were startling and straining with curiosity about the new, shorter beasts scattered around them. A few caresses and whispers from Abel, however, and the mares immediately quieted down. They began grazing after Abel helped us dismount.

I nearly stumbled and slipped on stones hiding under dewy moss because it was impossible to tear my eyes from the lovely flocks ahead. Like clouds floating in a green sky…no. "Like fluffy potatoes nestled among beans and broccoli," Hilda whispered behind me, reading my mind. I raised my eyebrow at her. She tipped her head innocently and winked.

I turned back to Abel and smiled. "You have a way with horses, I see."

Abel laughed. "I love all living things," he said, "and most living things respond well to love."

"Not all?"

"No," he replied with a note of sorrow, "not all. But come, and tell me why you are really here."

"You truly can see through people," I said. "I obeyed an impulse I had yesterday. You see," I continued in a rush, "I had never seen shepherds or sheep before, since they all had left the kingdom so long ago, and I had always heard about what shepherds and their flocks were like, and…" I shrugged. "I came today to find out. What it all is like."

"And you came to protect her?" he turned to Hilda with a mischievous grin.

She chuckled and swung an imaginary sword over

her head. "More likely, she would protect me. But I was sure Lady Judah would want to come. I decided she should not go alone, especially after her last journey, when she—" She stopped short, flushing, and glanced at me. "I mean—nothing. I came along for…companionship."

I frowned. Hilda had told me that she and Anna had long before agreed to not speak of that evil day unless it was absolutely necessary. Perhaps it was superstitious, but all three of us worried that speaking of the accident might somehow undo the healing wrought by the Enlightened One. Hilda mouthed, "Sorry," and kept walking.

Abel whistled a few notes. "It is always a good thing to have a companion for a journey, and you are also most welcome here."

"I am Hilda, by the way."

"Pleased to know you."

I caught up for the last part of the conversation. "And please, Abel, do me a favor and call me Judah. I feel rather silly about all the ceremony out here, in all this." I swept my hand over the flocks scattered around the valley.

"Thank you, Judah." Abel helped each of us down a particularly slippery spot. "Some places have a way of changing us, shifting how we see things. Ah, here they are, ladies."

And there they were—a hundred or so curly, frolicking, crying, floppy tiny lambs with their mothers, all carefully protected in rough pens fashioned from woven brush and branches. I gasped, rushing to the nearest fence.

"May we?" I begged, gesturing toward the sheep.

Abel grinned and offered a hand for us to climb over the improvised gate.

"I believe you mentioned wanting to learn about properly raising Jemimah?" Abel said. And then he taught us. Specifically, he showed Hilda and me how to care for a lamb by teaching what it meant to be a lamb and what it meant to be its mother. The hours, filled with wonder and laughter, marched by unnoticed. The only marker of time was a short break at noon. Colorful wool blankets were spread on the ground along with baskets of crusty bread, sharp sheep cheese, and bowls of sweet water. The shepherds invited us to join their simple meal.

Then it was back to the lambs.

I could have stayed there forever. It was late afternoon when Abel gently pointed out that Hilda and I should prepare for our journey home so we could arrive before dark. "May I accompany you?" he offered as he brought us to where, somehow, he knew our horses had wandered to rest.

I gazed to the sun for a moment. "Thank you, but I believe we will be fine, thanks to your noting the time sooner than we did." I rubbed Adara's neck with affection. The horses had been cared for well in our absence, and they seemed eager to run when Abel helped each of us mount. "I really don't know how to thank you. This day has been truly magical, for lack of a better word."

Hilda echoed the gratitude. She said later that she

would never forget that day.

"I hope you will come again." He looked me in the eyes. "You are always welcome." A few nearby shepherds called out farewells as we rode away. It was strangely difficult to head back into the forest, as though I was leaving something important behind.

"You are happier, my lady," Hilda observed, ducking to avoid a low-hanging branch. "I feel happier, myself. Maybe those delightful little creatures are more able to cheer the heart than all the revels of the kingdom. Maybe that's what made Grumwold such a great lady." She laughed. "She discovered that…that knitting with wool could cheer the heart, too, perhaps in a similar way as playing with sheep themselves."

"Maybe," I said. "Maybe."

CHAPTER 14

The morning after that first day in the valley, I glided out before dawn, this time alone. I had whispered my plan to Hilda before going to bed. Hilda wanted to go with me, but she was needed at the castle. Anna had been storming about Raven again, insulted that Raven had been asked to care for Jemimah and grumpy about covering for Hilda. Clearly, Hilda was needed to keep the peace on the home front.

The crisp morning air dispelled my mental fog. Adara headed toward the forest after a prod, galloping joyfully as if she, too, felt eager to return to the shepherds' valley.

Hours passed as minutes. The week had been full of wonders, but my mind settled on the shepherds and sheep. What made them special? Were they truly different from our farmers or herders?

Low-lying branches hugging the narrow forest road paused reflections, but finally the path widened, leaving space to think. What had Abel said? "Some places have a way of changing us." I shook my head to clear it of obstructions. *Be sensible, Judah—you're captivated by childhood stories come to life. There is no such thing as a mystical place, or special powers, or whatever fairytale magic old histories conjure. I am grown. If I can't see something, it doesn't exist. Besides, I'm sure I shall tire of everything by this evening.* Secretly, I hoped this was not true. I hoped beyond hope there was something in the valley, in the shepherds or the sheep, that really called my heart. I longed for…*transformation*. I couldn't understand it, but there was a quality my parents had, that Grumwold had—a quality I lacked. And my innermost being longed for it more than anything in the world.

I was near the edge of the forest where it dropped away to the valley below. Crashing in the bushes should have warned me, but it fell on my deaf ear. The bear was upon me like a mountain storm—sudden, swift, angry.

It was a huge, ferocious-tempered she-bear, one who must have been protecting cubs. She was rising to her towering height when I spotted her. A wayward breeze must have distracted Adara from sensing the bear until the same moment as I. She reared, screaming to the bear's roar, throwing me to the sky.

I jumped up—a weapon? Anything. I grabbed a large stick. "Adara." The horse had already bolted in terror with my weapons still attached to her saddle. I thrashed my stick wildly, but this made the beast angrier. She shook her massive head, saliva spraying, thundering the ground as she roared, swinging giant claws closer. "Abel." I screamed at the top of my lungs, hardly aware of what I was doing, "Help me. Help." *Oh, please—*

The bear rushed me.

My legs melted.

I fell on my knees. *Kill me quickly.* I closed my eyes.

But…the bear never reached me. Someone rose between me and the bear. A loud, trilling song like a bird sounded. Throaty growls filled the air.

I opened my eyes. A person. The bear grumbled and ambled away into the bush. The person turned, smiling, reaching out his hand to lift me.

"Abel?" I whispered, bewildered.

"You called for me," he said.

"You—you saved my life."

"You asked me to." He helped me to my feet, a steadying arm around my shoulder. "Easy, now."

"The—the—bear—"

"—is off with her cubs. Your horse is in the valley and will be fine. Are you all right?"

I still held his arm. "I—I think so." I started shivering, and Abel put his jacket around my shoulders.

"Sit back down for a minute. You are safe." Abel squatted next to me. "You did not hear the bear?"

"No." I squirmed.

"Why is that?" Abel's face remained kind, inviting trust.

I shrugged. "I…don't hear out of my left ear anymore." I avoided Abel's eyes. "Usually, it doesn't cause me grief."

"You did well to call for help."

I grimaced. "I don't think I even realized what I was doing." I shifted and laughed a little. "My attendants could tell you—calling for help is a sure sign that I've reached my limit. I do not easily ask for help."

"And why is that?"

"I am capable of taking care of myself." I shrugged. "I had independent parents. After all, stories say that my mother once co-led a massive army with my father, so how could I do any less than fend for myself?"

"Help is always there if you ask." Abel passed me an apple and water skin. "The people of the Mountain King wander these lands to provide aid, do they not?"

"How do you know about them?" I asked, surprised.

Abel laughed. "Some join us periodically for evenings by our fires."

"Well, if they're such a help everywhere, then why didn't they come when that…that beast was about to attack me just now?"

"You called for *me*," Abel replied.

I sniffed and shook my head against the terrifying memory. "I am feeling better now. Thank you." I stood and handed Abel the water skin. "How did you do that? It—it seemed to—to listen to you."

The moss was slippery, and I appreciated Abel's strong arm.

"Creatures respond if you communicate in a way they understand."

At this strange statement, I stopped and stared. "Are you being serious?"

"Yes."

"Will you teach me?"

"What do you want me to teach you?"

"How to do that. Communicate in different ways. Communicate with other creatures."

Abel smiled. "If you learn the ways of the shepherds, you will learn that, too. In fact," he shaded his eyes and gazed over the valley, "if you wish, later today, I will teach you a special song, one that only you will be able to hear. People also have their own ways of understanding. Learn your song well." The grassy path narrowed. "Then, like the bear, you will be able to understand without words. In time, you will learn to even sing the song." He regarded me with interest, pointing to the lambing pens. "But for now, are you ready to learn something new about sheep?"

I beamed. "What is it? Yes."

"Building fences." Abel laughed at my grimace. "Don't shirk now, Judah." He tugged the woven branches. "A solid fence in the only protection sheep have from wild animals and from themselves when the shepherd is not around. It is much more important than you think."

"Protection from themselves?" My eyebrows raised.

"Sheep are quite like people. They wander wherever their fancy or following leads them. If left to roam on their own without a boundary, they walk off cliffs, wedge themselves in gullies, get caught in a thicket."

I hadn't thought of that. "I suppose it is truth for humans, too, as you said."

Abel nodded for me to continue.

"It can be easy—and natural—for people to live in such a way that preferences, emotions, or reactions guide them rather than laws or even good sense or reason." I felt my cheeks grow warm. I was really talking about myself. "I—I can't say I always think through decisions carefully before acting." Mesda's form rose in my mind's eye.

Abel watched my face. "Mistakes make the heart heavy." He pointed to the necklace resting on my cloak. It must have flown out when I was hurled from Adara. "Someone loves you very much. A star diamond—the stone of a promise fulfilled."

I blushed. "Yes. It is beautiful."

"Who gave it to you?"

I fingered the jewel. "I was betrothed to someone from before my birth. He gave me the necklace."

"What do you think of him?" Abel offered me his water skin again.

I drank gratefully and wiped my mouth with the back of my hand like when I was a girl out with my father. We had not cared about ceremony in the woods. "It's complicated. My parents agreed to the betrothal, and until recently, I've always accepted it as a set reality. But I don't really know him, and the betrothal is more my parents' decision than…well, my own."

"And without your own choice…" Abel started.

"…is it really love?" I sighed. "See. It is complicated."

"In the end, the choice that will matter is your own, you know," Abel said.

"I suppose you're right." I picked up the sparkling

jewel. "Sometimes, I hold it up at night against the sky, and the light inside glows like a celestial being—" I broke off with a laugh. "But I don't need to bore you with my story."

Abel merely smiled, twinkling.

How did he do that with his eyes?

I blushed, straightening my shoulders. "How does one build a fence?"

~*~

I waved away Brunter, the head stableman, and brushed Adara myself that evening, whistling and relishing the solitude of dark stables. Then Hilda entered the stables and stopped short. She walked slowly around me, her eyebrows arched higher than I'd believed possible. "My lady, what happened? You—you look as though you wrestled a wild beast and lost." Not only did I smell like sheep and mud, but my hair was a curly birds' nest, clothes torn, hands and arms scratched, and burrs covering everything else. "Bath," she directed with a point.

I meekly complied but insisted first on snuggling my little Jemimah, and second, I inhaled a large snack. "Famished," I commented and then danced over to a tub filled with hot water. Singing and whistling bubbled out as I scrubbed. I remembered the special song Abel had taught me that day, the one only I would be able to hear. Although I knew the sound of it by heart, for some reason, I could not sing it. *How curious.* I shrugged and continued whistling another tune from childhood, splashing with happy abandon. I heard Anna and Raven join Hilda to mend the tears in my dress and cloak.

"You must have had a nice rustic day, my lady?" Anna commented, inquisitiveness resonating in her voice.

"I love being outdoors. I feel I've been confined for years since recovering from that fever," I sang from the other side of the screen. No further explanation, no defensiveness. This was very out of character, and I could guess what was going through the minds of my attendants— *What has gotten into the governor?*

Anna hmphed. "I hope you are planning to rest tomorrow?"

"Not while the weather is this nice. I'm afraid you'll just have to do without me for a bit. And I'm catching up on necessary work in the evenings."

"But the approaching war—"

"Kiran is working right now on that," I interrupted. "There is nothing we can do at present until he returns." There was no use arguing further, and Anna knew it.

"My lady, what on earth happened on your ride today?" Hilda's tone was sharp—she must have seen the most suspicious tear and stain from when I fell.

I couldn't put them off forever. Finally, I emerged in a luxuriously fluffy robe. "I was distracted at the wrong moment and took a tumble." I laughed at the shocked expressions on Hilda's and Anna's faces. "I won't do it again."

"You never fall from Adara." Anna gasped.

"As I said, I was distracted—you know how my hearing throws things off sometimes." No need to worry them. "Now, where is my adorable lamb?"

Anna hmphed again, and Hilda raised her eyebrows. Raven smiled a little without glancing up or saying a thing.

~*~

The third morning after I began visiting the shepherds in the valley found me with a carefully wrapped bundle strapped under my cloak. I had tried to replicate Abel's bundle when he brought the lamb to the castle as a gift. But my version was clumsier and less comfortable. Still, it sufficed, and Jemimah fell asleep as she lay huddled against me.

Abel laughed uproariously when he saw what I had done. Then he gazed at me, admiration and approval, on his face. "We'll make a shepherdess of you yet," he exclaimed. "Well done." His words pleased me more than I wanted to admit.

"I thought Jemimah would like a bit of air and sunshine, and perhaps some time with her own kind." I smiled with embarrassment. "I tried to remember how your bundle looked when you were at the castle, but I'm afraid my attempt isn't very good."

"Nonsense—it did the job marvelously. Well done."

I grinned. I wanted to jump and sing. "What is on for today? More fences?"

"Not with those beat-up hands. Give them a break.

Let me teach you why sheep need guiding in green pastures. There's a reason we can't let them run amok eating as much as they want. Then, you can learn about streams and places of rest."

"Only if you will let Jemimah and me play with the lambs first." I held out my hand playfully.

Abel shook it. "It's a deal."

And so, the week passed in sunshine, in fellowship, and then another week. I sensed my own budding transformation. I grew in health and strength. My heart filled with song. Anna and Hilda acted as though they barely recognized their previously dignified mistress, and officials of the court agreed fresh air and exercise did me a world of good. I spent most daylight hours with the shepherds and sheep, and Abel taught me the ways of the shepherd. There had never been a more beautiful, joyful time in my life.

"Do you believe in miracles?" Abel asked one afternoon, freeing a stone from a lamb's hoof.

I gazed up with surprise. "I believe in what I can see."

"Noncommittal." He handed me the lamb and smiled.

"What are miracles, anyway?" I buried my face in the lamb's soft wool. "This is a miracle."

"Yes. That is a miracle and more so than you realize. You accept this miracle because there is a part you can see and understand." He tapped on the ground with his staff. "A miracle is something beyond one's capacity for understanding, something greater and outside a scope of vision." Abel gently held out the shiny creature that had wriggled up toward his staff. "To this worm your very voice is a miracle. The color of the sky is a miracle. Its capacity for sound is limited to vibrations in the earth, and the closest it gets to experiencing color is sensing light and dark. Yet, here you are, speaking and singing, and there are the heavens in all blue majesty. Were it suddenly allowed the experience of song and sky, the worm would declare," he carefully placed the worm down again, "'it is a miracle.'" Abel watched me intently for a moment. "Even as the worm is, so is humanity. Yet many believe miracles do not exist."

His words echoed through my heart while I rode home that evening. Perhaps I was a worm slowly being given the gift of sight. Abel taught me to see life in new, beautiful ways, and I had much to think about.

CHAPTER 15

I lingered on my balcony, warm evening breezes brushing my face with the scent of flowers below. Closing my eyes, I sighed, the light of the stars in my mind as I leaned on the balustrade. A light touch fell on my elbow. I whirled to find the bright face of Kiran, and then I was folded in his arms. My heart leaped at his touch. My head spun.

"Kiran." I gasped once he released me. "When did you return?"

"Only just this moment, my lady," he said with a laughing bow. "I came to find my heart's desire as soon as I set foot inside castle walls."

"Kiran. Surely—" I stuttered and blushed.

"But surely, I am not mistaken? Surely," he took my hands and drew me close, "you feel something for me, dear Judah?" My name, caressed on his lips. He gently touched my cheek. What dry tinder awaited that spark. What flames erupted at a touch.

"I—I—" So this was love. And why not? The Mountain King's son had never come to me himself. Heart pounding, I raised my face for another kiss. Oh, blissful moment—

Finally, Kiran drew me to a nearby bench, reaching inside his shoulder bag. "I brought you something, my love," he said, drawing out a package wrapped in leather. He pulled the strap and revealed a box carved from stone. "Open it."

I lifted the lid. There lay a magnificent pendant on an intricate gold chain. The pendant, a precious stone of deepest black. It was as if a lake contained the midnight sky, and its shiny surface glinted reflection of balcony torches. I could see my own face mirrored on its perfectly smooth face. "Oh," I exclaimed, greatly pleased with the stunning piece.

"May I?" he asked, lifting the delicate chain.

"Of course." I breathed, bending so he could fasten the gift around my neck.

"Darling," Kiran chided in a teasing voice, "I really can't have you wearing the gift of another man, especially next to a gift from me. That would be improper."

"No—I suppose not," I replied, reluctantly tracing the star diamond's edge. The luminous piece made me feel more like royalty than a thousand attendants ever could. "I will put it away." I undid the clasp and handed the necklace to Kiran, who shut the piece up in the box that had held his gift. I took the box with me when we parted, promising to meet him in the morning to discuss his journey.

Flushed and flustered, I did not at first notice Raven playing with Jemimah on the bedroom floor. Raven stood in greeting, her eyes instantly riveted on the necklace I wore in place of the star diamond. "My lady," she gasped, "your necklace—"

"Isn't it striking?" I enthused, tucking the stone

box behind a tray of perfumes. "Kiran gave it to me. I've never seen the like."

"But, my lady, you were given a star diamond from the son of the Mountain King—his promise—"

"Yes, but he hasn't come, has he?" I snapped. "Frankly, I'm tired of waiting for a man who won't even tell me his real name, much less stop by for a visit."

"He is coming."

I whirled at the unfamiliar tone in Raven's voice, a rod of iron revealed in the normally-gentle attendant. Raven's eyes sparked. "Do not choose another."

I raised my eyebrow cooly, my fingers rubbing the cold stone. "Raven, you forget yourself." Who did she think she was?

Beware, Judah. Remember your mistake with Mesda.

Shrugging, I laughed and waved dismissively. "And goodness, so serious. This is just a necklace. I've not promised to marry anyone."

Raven opened her mouth to reply, but her words drowned in the entrance of Anna and Hilda.

"There you are." Anna rushed over, her face aglow. "Broden just surprised me, so I knew you must have seen Kiran has returned. But wait," Anna gawked at my necklace, "What is this?"

Hilda approached, and she, too, stared. "It's like a mirror," Hilda said, "only darker."

"It's stunning," Anna gushed. "It sets off your dark hair, contrasts your complexion, heightens your eye color. Who brought you such a perfect piece?" Her lips pursed, eyes mischievous, "…or do I even need to ask?"

"Kiran gave it to me just now." I did not look at Raven. "Yes, it was so romantic. No, I have not agreed to marry him. Yes, Hilda, I still have that necklace, but it's safe in a box. I really don't know. I don't have answers for that right now." Finally, I pled fatigue, shooed everyone out of the room, snuggled Jemimah absentmindedly for a minute, and went promptly to bed.

The next morning, I met with my advisors in the war council room. Kiran gave a full account of his journey, of the adventures he undertook to save the kingdom from attackers in the south.

"The end of it all is," he coughed, "I have managed to negotiate peace with the southern kingdoms."

A stunned silence fell across the room. Peace? Could there really be peace? Was this over without a single battle? "Do you mean terms of our surrender?" an older gentleman inquired.

"Or perhaps a temporary postponement?" a woman added from the side.

"No. I mean peace. The kingdoms have reversed their acts of aggression and are heading home even as we speak."

A pause settled at this declaration. Then cheers erupted with back-slapping and hand-shaking and congratulating all around, as if every person in the room claimed some level of responsibility for working the whole thing out.

I was the only one who, although speechless,

stared at Kiran with a raised eyebrow. The council had given him authority to begin negotiations with the southern lands, but how much had he made use of that authority? What had he done or traded to negotiate such peace? I hoped he had not promised any of our border towns or lands.

Kiran caught up with me as everyone left for the village square where I would announce the wonderful news. He held out his arm, and we walked together. "I saw your look in there, Judah. Ask what you will."

I frowned. "I confess that I feel uneasy, knowing that peace does not come without a price." I stopped and released his arm to face him, although my gaze dropped to his feet. "Kiran, I trust you with my life as you should know by now. But I am worried that—that you may have traded something important belonging to the kingdom to negotiate this peace." I looked up at him then.

He took my hand. "Say that again, dearest."

"I am worried that—"

"No," he interrupted, touching my chin, searching my eyes. "The other part. Would you, really, darling Judah? Trust me with your life?"

"Yes," I nodded.

"Then, Judah, I promise you, I did not give anything that was not already mine to give." He continued in the same serious tone. "Will you also trust me with that until this afternoon when we can talk further?"

The weight in my heart fell away like stones. "Yes, Kiran. You have relieved me greatly." I smiled up at him. "Now, please humor me in something. You will accept the reward I am about to bestow for your great deeds, won't you?"

"Anything you desire, my lady."

The villagers assembled in the square when the summons sounded, the crowd already large by the time Kiran and I ascended the platform. Children scrambled around the outskirts, chasing and laughing. Swelling chatter confirmed that rumors already flew faster than the hair and scarves whipping around this wild, windy morning. I stepped forward and waved the people to silence. The silence was full, expectant. Fear, courage, despair, determination—there had been no news these last weeks. Was there hope? Or a summons to war?

I cleared my throat. What a beautiful, beautiful throng of people, my people. *We were so close to losing some of you. So close to peril, possible destruction. So close to sorrow. But…* "Today, I bring you tidings of great joy," I began, my voice clear, strong, sharing news of peace.

Thunderous cheers rocked the square—no more threat of war. Peace and safety. Surely, all hearts swelled with gratitude toward the man who had saved their lives— Kiran. When I announced my reward for his great deeds—appointment as Head Councilor, a position vacant since Grumwold's death—it was impossible to rein in the wild enthusiasms.

Only one man did not cheer.

This man abruptly became the object of everyone's attention, for after my announcement, Raven appeared on the platform next to me. With power that none suspected she possessed, Raven's voice clapped like thunder over the crowd as she raised her arm toward the quiet man in the back.

"Behold, the son of the Mountain King."

The world around me became instantly silent. All eyes locked onto the man Raven had declared. Across the square, bearing a bundle of wool and a shepherd's staff, stood Abel.

Abel stopped and turned. His eyes fixed onto Raven's and then on mine.

A stunned moment passed. Then silence shattered as Kiran burst into laughter. He laughed and laughed. He was quickly imitated by all in the square. Rowdy comments flew back and forth.

"What's wrong with that woman?"

"Everyone already knows who that rather ugly man is."

"She's lost her mind."

"How embarrassing. Unless he put her up to the stunt?"

I did not laugh. Concern, embarrassment for my friends, confusion, all stormed through my mind, but no amusement. I shuffled Raven off the platform and into Hilda's care. "Have her lie down—perhaps she is feverish?" I whispered in her ear.

Kiran directed a narrow-eyed gaze toward Raven and then at Abel as he continued slowly down the street out of sight.

The unexpected moment broke up the assembly, and everyone headed home for celebrations. I slipped away before anyone could intercept me to find Hilda. Later, satisfied that Raven was resting, I went in search of Kiran. It was time to discuss his negotiations.

I found Kiran in the sunroom and joined him on the couch. "You have questions for me, Judah," he queried with a smile. "But first, a celebratory toast." Kiran poured wine. "To peace. And," he continued, raising his glass, "to a most beautiful, brilliant princess and thief, who has stolen not only my heart, but also the hearts of the people. Now, my lady—your questions."

"Yes." I put down my glass and hesitated. "I must know, I really must know the details of your negotiations with the southern kingdoms. What did you bargain to negotiate peace? What was the price?" I grabbed his free hand. "You did not trade off our land."

He slowly sipped his wine. "A sum of money was demanded, and I paid it."

"Money? How much? Where did you find the funds?" Had he promised what remained in the already depleted treasury brought low by war preparation efforts?

"I—now, you really must forgive me, dear Judah," he grinned. "I had my own resources, and I drew from them. That is all."

I sat back, dumbstruck. "You used your own funds to purchase our peace? Kiran—I—I don't know what to say. How much money did they demand?" What wealth could Kiran have to meet their demands? I leaned forward. "Tell me."

"Tell you what?"

"How much?" I gritted my teeth. "I must know—how much am I indebted to you?"

He then named a sum that extracted a gasp. Kiran put a finger over my lips as I began to protest. "Hush, darling. The money is nothing," he soothed.

Tears sprang out. "You really paid that sum—such a sum—from your own purse, Kiran? You would do such a noble thing for the kingdom? Why?"

Kiran took my hands. "I think you know why, Judah," he said, brushing my palm with his lips. I blushed, suddenly understanding as he leaned closer, whispering, "You know why…my queen." He stroked my face briefly and then kissed me fiercely.

"Kiran—" *He would do this for me. What amazing things will a man not do for love?* "Kiran." I was interrupted with a slow kiss, and then another. "How—how can I ever repay you? I cannot let you sacrifice yourself in this way." Although I longed to remain in his arms, I pulled myself away to look in his face. "I am indebted to you forever for this service you have rendered me, something which I could never repay."

"I am honored to serve my queen in any way possible—you must let it be so. I love you." Kiran drew me gently back. "But perhaps," he smiled and kissed my fingers one by one, "perhaps we will think of a way, someday…" He held my hand until I finally, reluctantly, stood to leave. "Meanwhile, if you will allow me," he held the glass of wine up to the light. "I have noticed that there are several positions in which I would like to place a few of my very capable men as a further service to this kingdom and its ruler."

"Kiran, you have but to ask."

"Thank you for your trust, Judah. As a start, I would like to place Broden as the new head justice, for he has extensive training in the arts of law."

I smiled. "As you desire, so do, Head Councilor."

"Thank you." Kiran bowed as I turned to go, and added just loud enough for me to hear, "My queen."

CHAPTER 16

I needed space to think. My balcony overlooked the gardens below, the Great River valley bordered by forests beyond. And past the forests were the shepherds with their flocks.

Shepherds. Abel. He must have been humiliated. Why else wouldn't he have visited the castle after the debacle in the square? Surely, he would have paid me a visit otherwise while he was in the village.

And Raven. Why had Raven made that wild proclamation? Was she truly ill? Or perhaps she was still angry with me about the necklace?

Tea sat untouched next to me. So much had occurred that day; my mind turned to more pressing matters. With peace within grasp, now I clung to renewed visions of a bright future for the kingdom. What would Grumwold have said about my appointments for new head councilor and head justice? Would the woman who held both roles for so many years have approved? Oh, that these two men would bring back the harmony that reigned under Grumwold's wise hand.

Justice was Grumwold's passion, her delight in life. As head justice, she ensured that those accused of wrong were treated fairly and only punished according to their deeds. She did not believe in keeping full prisons. "Work," she famously stated, "cures more ills and changes more hearts than merely rotting with the mice in confinement." Thus, when justice demanded, the convicted learned the value of hard work. This was never salted with cruelty. Rather, the work was useful: roads were developed, farmers received help in harvesting crops and plowing fields, fish were caught and shared with the poor, walls were repaired, and the elderly were cared for, all by the hands of the sentenced. Consequently, people began to see the convicted as fellow human beings who were learning to live life in a new way. When a sentence was completed, a previous criminal could expect to be welcomed back into regular life with open hearts and arms.

Although always humane, Grumwold developed a well-earned reputation of being discerning and tough. Grumwold's gifts of grace and mercy in no way diminished her enactment of justice. Those found guilty of having an unrepentant heart faced the most severe of penalties. Yet most hardened criminals found their punishments were tempered with grace. Grumwold herself would invariably come, quietly, with words of wisdom or understanding silence as needed, to help the convicted through their sentences. I had personally known her to sit for hours with a man or woman recently sentenced; and when some difficult physical task was put to them as punishment, Grumwold would be there, giving a hand. I am certain this practice, considered an eccentricity by her critics, won her the hearts of all the condemned. I firmly believe that no convict left her system of justice unchanged somehow for the better.

I sighed. The series of interim judges who took turns filling the job since Grumwold's death had done their best, but it was time for people with vision to step in, bring back the glory of Grumwold's days. May Kiran and Broden be the people for today.

The view—and with those pleasant memories—wrought serene magic for my mind. Now I had work to do to formalize the new positions.

I waited until the following day to tell Anna of the promotion. She shrieked, alternately dancing around the room and hugging me. In between hugs, I gathered up my pet lamb and bundled the increasingly heavy dear for a short ride. Anna's ecstatic reaction didn't surprise me in the least—not only was this a great honor granted her favored man, but it was also a patriotic position. Anna has always considered duty to one's country of primary importance in life. She would be especially proud of this promotion. I was sure of it. Broden, hopefully, shared Anna's patriotic idealism if he wished to continue in harmony with her.

I shrugged and braced myself for a verbal torrent praising Broden's shining attributes, a river of words flooding my ear as Anna followed me out the door. It was time to check on Raven, who was kept in a quiet part of the castle while recovering from this apparent brain fever. "Broden is so level-headed and quite brilliant. He will be a perfect head justice. He has carefully studied all the laws set in place by Grumwold eons ago, and he has even created some additions that will expand the detailed applications and consequences for the laws already in place."

"Ah. Well. How lovely." I comprehended only the gist of Anna's prattle as we proceeded to the attendants' apartments. Jemimah wiggled in my arms. I hardly knew my way around this part of the castle. Beyond my childhood exploring, had I ever visited the apartments of people who served at the castle? No, other than that awful day of Mesda's death. I shivered.

"And here we are." Anna knocked gently and opened the door at Hilda's voice bidding us enter. There sat Raven, knitting with Hilda, drinking tea in the waning light of the evening. A few lit torches provided light necessary for their labors. The women smiled pleasantly. Hilda put down her work. Raven continued to knit. Anna, surprisingly, nodded cordially to Raven.

"Such beautiful work you ladies are doing, worthy of the lovely wool which we received so generously." I smiled broadly. *Oh no—don't talk about anything that could bring Raven back to the topic of Abel.* I coughed discreetly and changed the subject. "I brought Jemimah to keep you company." I unwrapped the growing lamb. But this, too, linked to the shepherd who had been such a cause of uproar.

Raven stood and gazed deeply in my eyes. "You must believe me about the son of the Mountain King," she said. "I tell you only the truth, as I always have done." Her voice, though quiet, was as powerful as that first day she entered the castle halls.

I coughed again, clearing my throat uneasily. "Ah, yes—" I trailed off. "You have been working so hard, Raven, and it is good for you to take a rest." I looked to Hilda and Anna for help, but they avoided eye contact, suddenly occupied with knitting and petting the lamb. "A rest to—to keep your mind quiet for a while," I finished.

Raven watched me.

I shuffled my feet. "Well, I must leave now. There is so much to do with—well—everything—please, keep Jemimah here for the evening for company." I paused at the door. "Hilda—a moment?"

Hilda joined me out in the corridor. "How is Raven?" I whispered.

"She seems perfectly normal, my lady. She talks about almost nothing beyond the Mountain King and his son, but that is not unusual for her." Hilda teared up. "All I can believe is that she is sincere and must be, somehow, operating under a delusion that shows every semblance of truth to her mind."

"I feel the same way." I paced the corridor.

"My lady, another thing I am worried about more than Raven alone." Hilda's whisper paused me in my tracks. "What about Abel and the other shepherds?" Hilda clenched her fists, her knuckles turning white. "Surely, no one would show his face again after such a humiliation. What if he never comes back? What if they leave the kingdom again, for good?"

"The same thoughts entered my mind," I took Hilda's hands, "which is why not three hours ago, I dispatched a messenger to Abel. I apologized profusely for the embarrassment caused by Raven's outburst and begged him to not be a stranger to the castle henceforth. I felt torn when he met my gaze there in the square." I massaged my forehead. "We can only hope the messenger made it in time. Meanwhile," I gave Hilda a brief hug, "I thank you, from the bottom of my heart, for looking after Raven."

Hilda wiped away traces of tears, nodded, and guided me back to a familiar part of the castle before returning to Raven.

The door to my apartments stood ajar. Was that music coming from inside? There, an unexpected peaceful scene: Kiran in my sitting room, playing a lute, singing softly. A servant had placed a dining table inside, and flames crackled in the fireplace, setting the room aglow. Tension in my neck and shoulders released like a cord.

I accepted a glass of wine, gratefully sinking into a soft chair. Kiran winked and continued playing and singing, the contrast between his golden head and dark eyes set off by sparkling light. I could get used to this every evening. The realization startled me. What did that mean? Was this the direction life was going to take, and this the man to grace my years? This did not seem tedious. On the contrary, it was delightful.

I gazed into the undulating firelight. Finally, Kiran put aside the lute and stood, gracefully offering his arm. "My lady, if I might be so bold as to give you a quiet dinner in your private apartments."

I smiled

"I did not want to presume, but here I am," he

continued. "I thought if only I could compel a certain hardworking princess to enjoy a relaxing evening with me?" He kissed my hand, drawing a blush to my cheeks as I sat.

"Thank you." I chuckled. "You curing me makes you a type of physician, and I suppose I must obey the physician's orders. And what a difficult regimen you've prescribed." I sniffed appreciatively. When had I last eaten that day? He was so thoughtful and had even prepared some of my favorite dishes.

The servant remained to wait on us. As we ate, Kiran regaled me with tales of his adventures on the recent journey. For my part, I encouraged his tales while carefully avoiding sharing any of my own. How could I tell him I spent almost every possible moment while he was gone in the company of the shepherds? With Abel, especially? The thought of Abel brought a slight smile. I lost the thread of conversation and glanced up.

Kiran was watching me.

After the final course, I suggested enjoying dessert near the fire. The closer seating arrangement would allow for cozy tête-à-tête.

Kiran and I settled on the couch and raised the wine in toast. A knock sounded on the door, and one of Kiran's men entered and bowed hastily, requesting an immediate audience with the head councilor.

Kiran apologized and left the room.

Minutes passed.

I caught my fingers tapping the cushions impatiently. What could be taking so long? Had something happened?

Finally, the door opened. I was startled at the grave look on Kiran face, nearly spilling my wine. "Kiran. What has happened? Why do you look so?"

Kiran glanced at me and then his eyes returned to the flames. "Judah, where did you send a messenger this afternoon?" he asked.

I tried to not show my astonishment. "Why—I—just sent a message to a friend. Nothing of importance." Why was I acting so hesitant? Why did I not want to tell him that it was a message to Abel? "Why do you ask?"

Kiran watched me, shrugged, and sighed. "Overly cautious, I suppose, after the news I just received—"

"What is it? You frighten me, Kiran."

He leaned forward, taking my hand. "Darling, I left one of my men behind to keep an eye on the eastern side of the kingdom. He has just sent a message of a most disturbing nature."

I could not breathe. What had happened?

He stood, pacing the room before continuing. "I have received a direct, irrefutable report that one of your own attendants, she who is called Raven, is not actually suffering from a brain fever or anything else." He paused and slammed his fist into his hand. "She is an agent for the southern kingdoms, tasked with breaking the negotiated peace. Her goal? Instigate an internal rebellion to weaken this kingdom for an eventual invasion."

The words fell like lead. I leaped up, hardly aware of my actions. How could this be? That would make

Raven a traitor of the worst kind. "No, Kiran, Raven can't be." I bowed as the gravity of the situation dawned on me. "I am sure, very sure, that she is suffering under a belief that what she said in the square was true, no matter how ridiculous it appears to us all. But she cannot be a…a traitor."

"Darling, this is a shock—please sit—compose yourself." Kiran signaled for water. I drank gratefully. "I can hardly believe the news myself, and if it weren't for the unassailable nature of the source…" Kiran groaned and shook his head. "I'm afraid, darling, that is not all." He took my hand.

"What else can there possibly be?" I whispered, staring at the fire. "No, that will not do—" I was a governor and a princess. I could not give in to common weakness. I shook myself. "Tell me everything. I must know the worst if that is not yet the worst."

"What is worse," Kiran said, his voice rising with anger, "is that Raven is not committing her traitorous deeds alone. She is working in league with someone whom I have only just learned received the benefit of this castle's friendship and lands—"

I gasped. *Please, no.*

"—the shepherd who is considered the chief, a man called Abel."

"But that's impossible." I covered my mouth, fighting dry sobs.

"Why?" Kiran's reply was sharp. He stared keenly.

"Because…" I closed my eyes. What to say? "Because that would make absolutely no sense. If

Raven and the shepherd are secretly working together for the southern kingdoms, why would Raven herself have identified her partner agent and named him as the son of the Mountain King?"

Kiran suddenly chuckled as he squeezed my hand. "Because, my innocent dove, the nature of war is more convoluted that you know. The enemy is not the southern kingdoms. The true enemy is the one sponsoring and directing the southern kingdoms—the Mountain King himself."

"No." My voice was stronger than I intended. "I will not—cannot—believe that."

"Judah," Kiran's voice remained soft, "you do not know the circumstances of your parents' fall, do you?"

My jaw dropped. Could he possibly have information about the mystery surrounding my parents' past?

"Your parents—it was the Mountain King who deposed them and banished them from their thrones and palace." Kiran leaned closer. The firelight glowed on his hair like a burning wheatfield. "It was all his doing. And the shepherds themselves were in league with the Mountain King. That is why they left."

The foundations of my world shuddered, cracked—the earth itself trembled at Kiran's words. "Why?" I choked out.

"Jealousy," he replied. "He couldn't stand the thought of your good parents expanding their kingdom and ruling with power that rivalled his own." Kiran threw a stick in the fire. "So, he destroyed them, leaving them mere managers of a kingdom where they had once ruled as king and queen." He looked back at me. "Now the Mountain King is ready to finish the work he started and crush with finality the offspring of the couple who dared defy his tyranny. He is going to use your own people, Judah, to ruin you forever."

"How?" My whisper was barely audible above the crackling fire.

"By the most effective manipulation imaginable. He will inspire your people to align themselves with a personality so revered that they would abandon anyone—even you—to follow him— the son of the Mountain King."

"But—I—why would he do that? We were betrothed before I was even born. The man has sent me lavish gifts and messages for years."

Kiran regarded me shrewdly. "Ah, but have you ever met him yourself?"

I flushed. "No."

"So, you're taking for truth and fact the words of someone you've never met, someone who, for all you know, may be nothing but a fictitious creation of the Mountain King for the purpose of manipulating you to believe and do whatever he says." Kiran paused. "Are you telling me you believe something you have never seen?"

My throat was dry. My heart hammered in my chest. "I have never thought of it that way. But," I clung to a thought with the strength of the desperate, "why should he not exist? Why would the Mountain King make up such an elaborate hoax, complete with betrothal promises, gifts, and letters, and everything else? What purpose would that accomplish?"

Kiran waved his hand as if brushing away cobwebs. "The oldest desire in the book, sweet lady. Pure lust for power drives a person to many things. The Mountain King is a despot. To secure his hold on power, he had to make your parents—and then you—believe that he was actually on their side and yours. Then he could manipulate you as he wished. What better way to accomplish this than to fabricate an elaborate betrothal scheme that supposedly aligns you with him and effectively purchases your affection? And by creating a loving son character to star in the story, the Mountain King provided a relatable central figure whom the masses would unquestionably adore and follow. By making up a son, he has you, and he has them."

Kiran took a drink. Lowering the glass, he continued, "But look at the facts. The supposed son conveniently hasn't condescended to show his face in these parts, so no one knows what he looks like, if he even exists. The beauty of this treacherous plan is that the Mountain King could have any number of possible characters waiting in the wings to present as the real ruler for the people. The Mountain King can put the plan of son-turned-rescuer into action whenever he feels the time is right. Apparently," Kiran snapped his fingers, "now is his moment. Whoever this Abel truly is, he and Raven have played out the Mountain King's plan so perfectly that pure chance enabled me to ruin it yesterday—for the time being." Kiran rubbed his forehead and grimaced. "If I hadn't been present to ridicule the moment Raven chose to present a false son of the Mountain King and claim him as the rightful ruler of the kingdom, one surrounded by enemies and ready for his strong army to come and rescue everyone from all evil, who knows what would have happened…" Kiran's words died out.

My eyes grew wide. "What can be done?"

"There is only one thing I can and must do."

My tears pierced the floor. "What is it?"

"I must order the arrest and trial of Raven and Abel as traitors and spies."

CHAPTER 17

The back door closed slowly, silently. I glided to the secret gate in the castle walls, a moonlit figure shrouded in a dark cloak. The valley spread wide and still before me with the river glistening far off below the moon. Though I had traveled this way so many times, I could barely make out the bridge. I hurried. Time was precious, but the journey to the forest was achingly longer in the dark.

I halted at the edge. Would this plan work? Had I come all this way for nothing? I stepped forward, finding the familiar path, but quickly lost all sight as the moon hid behind branches.

"Hello?" I jumped at the shaky sound of my own voice. What else should I say? Dare I call louder? "Hello?" Still nothing. *Please hear me.* I tried again. "Is anyone there? I need help from the Mountain King."

Instantly, I sensed rather than saw a form materialize in the darkness. A woman's voice called softly. "Greetings, Lady Judah. How may I be of service to you?"

"You are one of the Mountain King's people who guard the land?"

"I am."

I almost cried in relief. My plan had worked. "I

have an urgent message for the shepherd called Abel who keeps his flocks in the closest northeastern valley."

"I know him."

"The message pertains to matters of interest to the Mountain King. Will you make sure it is delivered to Abel this night? I dare not go myself, not tonight."

"It shall be done, Lady Judah, even as we finish speaking." She slipped the sealed paper into her cloak.

"And," I hesitated, "will you add a verbal message that I will wait all night in my apartments with my candle lit, looking for a return messenger?"

"Even so, it shall be done."

I described how to access the castle's secret gate and the path below my balcony. I would listen for a signal.

The woman nodded.

"I thank you, thank you, from the depths of my heart." I breathed, but the woman was gone. Time for the long walk back to the castle. It was too late to save Raven. Kiran had immediately secured her in a locked room guarded by his own men, but I could at least warn Abel of the danger he was in. Stumbling through the darkness, I wondered why I was risking everything to warn Abel after all I had been told earlier that evening. Why was I choosing to remain loyal to him after all the logical reasoning Kiran put before me and all the evidence against the Mountain King? Was it because Abel was loyal to the Mountain King? But why should I trust Abel, who might be a spy? *Because I know Abel. I don't know how, but I do know him. And I know he is who he says he is—a shepherd, not a traitor.* I startled myself with the intensity of this conviction and quickened my pace. I shouldn't be gone too long.

I had told Kiran I was going for a walk to ponder everything and especially to consider the proposal of marriage he whispered in my ear that evening by the fire. It seemed wise to not risk inquiry by taking too long for my supposed breath of fresh air.

Marriage. I could not deny the thought had whispered through my mind more than once in recent weeks. What should I do? Kiran was handsome and dashing, and what a brilliant match for the governor to marry the Enlightened One. He made me feel special, beautiful, like a queen.

I tripped on a stone. A queen. *I could become a queen if I married him. It is my birthright.* Kiran would help me claim the throne for my own. My heart pulsed faster. I smiled, held my head higher. But there, a twinge of…what? Conscience? Caution? By then I had arrived at the secret gate, and I concentrated on entering like an apparition of the night.

It was not until my bedroom door finally closed behind me that I sighed with relief. A light had been left burning. I placed it in the open window for the nightlong vigil. I warned Abel in my note that he was in imminent danger of being accused and tried as a spy along with Raven and begged that he take temporary cover. Now to wait for his reply. It would be several hours at least before a messenger could slip into the castle through the gate that I had left unlocked.

I passed the first few hours pacing the room,

knitting, sketching, watching the stars. Everything on me was coated in a fine layer of dust from the walk, but I did not want to risk a bath—what if the messenger arrived and I didn't hear? Then impatience set in. Why had Abel not yet sent someone? Had he received the message? My legs burned after the mad speed in the dark. I finally rested my throbbing head on the day couch near the window so I could watch the fire.

The long night passed. As dawn tore across the sky, I cursed myself for not delivering my own message and demanding a course of action directly from Abel. *This is what comes from relying on someone else, even if that person was a servant of the Mountain King.* I had intended to tell the return messenger about the early morning trial scheduled in which Raven would be accused and sentenced, but now it was too late. "You have failed me," I whispered, tears of frustration dragging stripes down my cheeks. Would Abel hide in time? Was there any way to save Raven? Our system of government had been set in such a way that whatever the chief justice decreed held true—not even the governor could overturn it. And the new head justice was Kiran's man.

The maid who brought morning tea found me at the window, staring at the sunrise. I could almost feel deep circles discoloring the skin under my eyes. Dust lay everywhere. My hair was a mess, and my clothing showed stains from the previous night's tromp. The servant discreetly coughed, left the tea, and ran, probably in search of my attendants, someone who could make me dignified in time for the trial.

"My lady. What on earth—" Anna gasped upon entering the room at Hilda's heels.

Hilda ruthlessly kicked her. "Anna…" she warned.

Anna raised her eyebrows and shrugged.

Like a hurricane, they whipped through the hundred details to prepare a governor for a formal public event. I remained still, a boulder in their storm, silent and withdrawn. I didn't care. Hilda's grim mood seemed to match my own.

Anna, however, was perky and chatty enough for all three of us. She appeared pleased about the upcoming events. She had never liked Raven. Perhaps she now justified her dislike, as if she'd had a sixth sense about Raven being a traitorous spy. Anna began to say it was a good thing she had never accepted the woman into her own confidences, but a severe look from Hilda quickly shut her up. She huffily switched to the weather. Eventually, the morose atmosphere dampened even Anna's chattering, and she finished her work in silence.

"There, my lady—you look perfectly presentable now." Anna gave a satisfied smiled as she and Hilda stepped back to survey their handiwork. I did not spin around for them as usual, but thanked them absently.

"Hilda, a word with you, please," I said as the ladies opened the door to leave.

Anna raised her eyebrow and then walked out, closing the door behind her.

My conversation with Hilda lasted until the latest

possible moment, and Anna had to send two different servants to collect me in time for the trial.

The courtroom was damp with morning air. Head Justice Broden settled, obviously self-satisfied, into his judge's chair. Anna would have puffed with pride at the dashing figure he cut in the dark robes of justice. Anna, however, had decided against attending the trial, claiming she had a headache.

I felt alone even though sitting between Kiran and Hilda. I wished Abel were here with me. The thought flashed with the fierceness of lightning. I glanced at Kiran. Had I spoken it aloud? But Kiran merely pressed a smile into place and took my hand. I, in turn, took Hilda's, gripping it as a lifeline. She was pale. We both knew the direction this trial could take.

The old double-doors of the courtroom groaned opened like dying thunder, and Raven was led inside. She was dressed in white as always, a snowy pillar with purity belying denunciation. This time, she stood handcuffed like a criminal. Her eyes found mine, and she smiled in a way that broke my heart.

Hilda cried quietly.

The accused was left in the middle of the room, facing the judge.

The trial began.

My heart ground like a miller's stone. I could hardly hear the accusations brought by Kiran's men, swearing they had seen and heard Raven betraying secrets to the enemy and plotting a rebellion from within the village itself, set to spread throughout the kingdom.

Evidence piled high; a rock wall mounded around the accused.

Raven never uttered a word in her own defense.

She was accused of plotting with, aiding, and abetting the enemy, a traitor to the kingdom.

The judge left the room to consider the evidence again. Heavy silence. It was as though we lay buried, crushed under the silent weight of earth. How was it that mere air could press with the power of stone? No one looked at the accused save Hilda and myself. When Raven's gaze moved to us, we smiled encouragingly, albeit tearfully. Right before the door opened to readmit the head justice, I glanced at Hilda and nodded my head. We were ready.

Broden cleared his throat. "In light of the heavy evidence and subsequent conviction as a traitor to the land and spy for the enemy," his hands twitched.

My heart plunged.

"I sentence you, Raven, to death."

She never even flinched.

Then Hilda and I rose as one person and stepped to the floor in front of Raven to kneel before the judge in the pose proper for appeals.

"Your Honor," I cried out, "hear our petition—listen to our request."

CHAPTER 18

I hoped Hilda wouldn't keel over as she knelt next to me before all those people in the courtroom. When we spoke together before the trial, Hilda declared she wouldn't have the courage to request mercy for her friend if she hadn't believed Raven's innocence as strongly as she believed the sun would rise. Now, Hilda trembled like a bird.

The court froze.

An eternity passed.

"Permission to speak," Head Justice Broden finally replied. His fingers drummed on the bench.

Hilda and I stood.

I cleared my throat. "Your Honor, the writer of the laws of the land was my teacher and friend, and I am sure it is no surprise to you that I, too, am as familiar with the law as with my own hand." I paused for a breath and gazed toward Raven for a moment before turning back to the head justice. Broden's eyes glinted as he watched me intently. "I know that if a person—any person—has been convicted of a crime for the first time in this country and that person has the support of at least two non-family witnesses who have had consistent contact with the accused and who can vouch for the good character of the accused, then a sentence of death must be commuted." I spoke with a power that bore proof of my royal blood. I pointed at Raven. "I, Lady Judah, governor of the land, stand as witness to vouch for the good character of this woman."

It was Hilda's time. She squared her shoulders. "I, Hilda, attendant to the governor, also stand as witness to vouch for the good character of the accused."

There. And now our plan must work. It must.

If my eyes were steel blades, I'd have used them to pin the head justice to the wall. I grew taller inside as my voice rang out. "I stand now upon the law and call for the sentence to be banishment from these lands."

Kiran scowled, and the judge glared disapproval. We stood on a knife's edge. All around the courtroom, however, people nodded their approval. Broden must know that there was nothing he could do in the face of the law and the people. He glanced uneasily at Kiran and picked up his gavel. "Request granted. The convicted is sentenced to lifelong banishment to the far southern lands, never to return on pain of death." The gavel slammed, finality echoing around the room as if the head justice were eager to settle the thing before anything else happened. "The sentenced will be escorted by guard out of the country."

Hilda's next cue. This was her difficult part to play in whatever drama would unfold from here.

I looked pointedly at her.

She stepped forward. "Your Honor," she said, her voice trembling slightly.

"Yes?" Broden barked.

"I request permission," her voice grew and rang,

"to fulfill the right of a lady convicted of a crime and banished, to have among her escort a protector of her choosing."

Broden raised his eyebrow and looked to Kiran again. The latter frowned and finally, grudgingly nodded.

Broden cleared his throat. "Granted, if you are the person chosen by the convicted for the position of protector."

For the first time, Raven's voice resounded through the courtroom. "I choose her."

It was settled. My heart slammed. Our lives were about to drastically change. Hilda gripped my hand.

Another nod from Head Justice Broden and the guards came to escort the prisoner from the room.

"Wait," Raven's voice echoed the second time.

Everyone stopped. "I have one thing I must say." She turned to a surprised Kiran and raised her chained arms to point at him. "This man is a deceiver, and soon, he will be the cause of much suffering in the land."

Her words struck a blacksmith's final blow. Kiran leaped up and pounded over to Raven, frowning fiercely.

He spat in her face. "Be gone, witch. You are the one who has deceived the people, and you have worked your deception long enough."

"I leave, but not at your command." Raven, looking Kiran in the eyes, dropped her voice so that I could barely hear. "I know what is coming." She turned and left the court with her guards.

There was not much time before the enforced departure. Hilda hurriedly packed for herself and for Raven. I helped as much as I could. Anna was no help at all, having gone into hysterics when she received the news that Hilda was leaving her in order to aid "that woman."

"It's not a permanent thing, dear Anna," I had tried to reassure her. "Hilda will accompany Raven on the journey and remain for a time to help her settle. Eventually, she will return to us." But I think we all knew inside Hilda would be absent for several months or more. I worried about Anna. What would she do without her level-headed friend around? What would I do?

I tried to hide tears by scurrying around collecting warm clothing and ordering food provisions for the journey.

That afternoon Hilda rode out with Raven and a guard, carrying her sword, shield, and a precious parting gift from me: Jemimah, tucked snugly under her cloak. The dearest thing I had, I sent to comfort them. I'd insisted that Anna wouldn't have time to help care for the lamb, but I think Hilda knew better.

And perhaps—the thought was a strange one—perhaps I believed the lamb would be safer with them. But why? I only knew I was uneasy.

As I watched the departure from my window, tears streamed down my face.

Hilda raised her hand in farewell and blessing.

I wondered at what I had done. *I hope this is the right thing. Abel, what would I not have given for your counsel last night. Kiran will probably be angry with my interference. But an argument is worth saving Raven.*

I returned Hilda's farewell blessing, wiping my eyes.

Anna had fled to her chambers. Now the silence lay like a fog. Hilda would be missed by everyone. She had joked about being the only truly sensible person around, and she was right.

Raven might not be missed by all, but despite our different views on certain topics, I had come to rely on her quiet wisdom. She noticed things that others didn't. Marah felt somehow less safe without her. Regardless of the seemingly irrefutable evidence presented against her, something was not right. There must have been a mistake.

On this hope, Hilda and I had built our bold plan to save Raven from death. Raven had to be innocent, as was Abel. Perhaps Kiran had been deceived. "We need a miracle," I whispered.

The riders faded from view. I informed a servant I was tired and not to be disturbed under any circumstance until the following morning. Then I locked my door. It was time to prepare.

Abel had not sent someone to me, so I would go to him.

I sneaked out of the castle again that evening, but this time with Adara and a blackout lantern. My night ride would take me deep into the woods and beyond.

When I arrived a few hours later at the first valley, the shepherds and flocks were gone.

My message had warned Abel to hide, but I hadn't

expected him to disappear completely with the other shepherds and flocks. I dismounted to stand at the edge of the woods, hardly believing my eyes. Although night had arrived, a full moon lit the valley. It was unmistakably empty. Could Abel have left without even saying good-bye? What was I going to do? Dropping to the ground next to Adara, I buried my face in my hands.

A solution flashed, a beacon to light my way. But it was so simple that I wondered at my own obtuseness. Startling Adara, I leaped up and—for the second night in a row—called out for the help of the Mountain King's people. A cloaked man approached me in the darkness.

"Greetings, Lady Judah. What assistance can I render you?"

"The shepherds. Abel is not here. I must speak with him."

"They have moved, lady. The shepherds are in the next valley east of here. Come. I will guide you on the path. It is not far."

The relief flooding me was so great that I wondered at myself. The next valley was smaller and rockier, requiring careful footing.

There, on a broad, flat boulder, stood Abel.

He immediately moved to meet me as if he had known I would come. I almost cried with relief at his approach. *Why does my heart leap and pound now that I am with him again?*

"Greetings, Judah. You are welcome." Even in the dark, his eyes sparkled. I suddenly felt shy as Abel helped me down from Adara, leading me to the boulder to sit and talk. "It has been some time since you visited us." There was no accusation in his voice, only kindness and invitation.

"I have missed you." My words formed before I had a chance to stop them.

"You have something on your mind," Abel noted.

I nodded and sniffed, embarrassed as the stress and sorrow of the day welled up, overflowing in the relief of tears. Once talking, I found myself pouring out my mind to him, how the return of Kiran distracted me from my visits, how embarrassed I was about Raven's behavior that day in the square, how awful I felt about Raven's sentence and how certainly there was a mistake. I related how I missed the guiding wisdom of Grumwold and wished for those earlier days. "Why didn't you reply with a message last night? I stayed awake all night waiting, and no one ever came. Did you not receive my message?"

"I did receive your message, and I came to talk with you. I sang below your window the song I taught you that no one else can hear, but although your light was lit, you did not come out."

"How could that be? I—" I stopped short as it dawned on me. "I lay down because I was tired of standing, and…and I must have lain on my good ear." I tried to swallow the lump in my throat and moaned. "You risked your life to come all that way last night, and I did not hear you because I…I turned my deaf ear to you." I touched his hand and whispered, "Can you forgive me? I am sorrier than I can say."

"There is nothing now to forgive." His tone caressed.

"Thank you." I hesitated. "Abel, there is something else I must speak with you about that weighs on me." I told him all that Kiran had relayed to me, including the information about my parents and the Mountain King and his son and described the accusations brought against Raven and Abel himself. "It seems so horrible and ridiculous, and the fact that it could be true terrifies me."

"What do you know to be the truth?" Abel asked.

"I—I don't know. There is so much I do not know of my own history, mysteries that my parents never revealed to me. The Mountain King himself is shrouded in mystery. I don't want to believe what is said about Raven, but I do not know. I do know, though, although I don't understand why, that you are not a traitor. Somehow, I know that anything you do would be…good." Softly I added, "That is why I had to warn you. I think that is why I have come."

Abel suddenly changed the subject. "What has happened to your necklace, Judah? Where is the star diamond, the promise you wore?"

Surprised, I stared at him. What did that have to do with anything?

Abel sat in expectant silence, watching me. I reluctantly told him about the marriage proposal I had received the previous night, how the necklace I wore was from the man who had proposed to me, the man who was my head councilor. I had put the other necklace away. "I cannot wear both necklaces at once, you know."

"But are you not already promised to another?" he probed.

I glared at him, at his words, flaring with an anger I didn't understand. How dare he? "I am perfectly free to make my own decisions—I belong to no man." I raised my head, haughty. "And who do you think you are with the right to inquire into my personal affairs? Who are you to tell me what I ought to or ought not to do? Am I not of royal blood, with the right to choose my own husband?"

"You are of royal blood, and you were given the right to choose your own husband."

"Then I thank you for staying out of my personal business."

"Do you truly wish to be united to this man?" Abel persisted as if he had not heard me.

"If I wish it, I shall do so." I stood abruptly. "I thank you for your time. I must be going." In my fury, I tripped on the boulder edge and only Abel's quick, strong arm kept me from falling and injuring myself. Further incensed by embarrassment, I shook off his arm, stumbled to my horse, and departed without a word of farewell.

CHAPTER 19

After caring for Adara, I sneaked up the back stairway to my apartments, determined to not waken anyone in the castle. So, of course, I was shocked to find Kiran waiting in my sitting room.

He turned from the fire and moved quickly to me with his hands outstretched. "There you are, darling. I've been worried something terrible happened to you."

"Kiran, I—I'm fine. Why aren't you asleep?"

"Like I said, I was so worried. Someone saw you riding off, but there was no news of your return. Anna left the door to your sitting room open when she went to bed and didn't think you would mind if I waited here. Come, my darling. Surely you are happy to see me."

He embraced me and then held me at arms' length, bending down to look in my face. "Where on earth have you been, my queen?"

Flustered and tired after the long ride, I did not reply for a moment.

"Judah?" he persisted.

I had not been looking forward to talking with Kiran after the trial that morning. I had thwarted what he believed to be a proper enactment of justice, and now had just returned from fraternizing with the enemy, as I was certain he would view my visit with Abel. Discussing the matter could spark what surely would turn into our first major disagreement, something I didn't have the spirit for at the moment. I finally replied, smiling. "My heart was heavy after such a horrible day with the trial and everything. I needed a ride to clear my head."

"That was quite the ride." He studied my face.

"It was quite the trial," I shot back.

"Darling, you have had such an ordeal this day, and after the shock of last night's horrible news, too." Kiran's voice shifted, now sweet and tender. "No wonder you feel exhausted. You must have ridden through the woods?" He continued to scrutinize my face, pulling a leaf from my hair.

I remained silent.

"Well, I know what you need, my queen. Sleep long and deeply, get your rest. Tomorrow, at noon, I have arranged for a special, private banquet for us to enjoy together."

I raised my eyebrows. "How thoughtful of you, Kiran. And by private, you mean…?"

"Alone." Kiran kissed me on the forehead. "I hope we may discuss a certain proposal together."

As he exited, I called him back. "Kiran."

He turned, his hand on the door. "My sweet?"

"You aren't angry with me? About this morning?"

Kiran laughed. "My love, you forget that I like it when your feisty side comes out." With a wink, he was gone.

I was so, so tired. Mind, body, spirit groaned. I was as a dry creek bed whose waters had ceased, left with cracked mud and grasses tossing about in the wind. Instead of falling at once onto my bed, though, I opened the window and sat watching the stars as if they could pour water onto that parched ground. *My parents, why did you not tell me everything? What secrets do you still keep? Grumwold, you told me much after their death, but even you did not tell me everything.*

I recalled what Grumwold said about the events leading up to the Destruction and the departure from Amia, but there had been no mention of royalty. And perhaps out of deference to my parents, Grumwold had not described the motives behind the rebellion other than, "they were advised by a hasty association with a persuasive councilor to rebel against the rule of the Mountain King, forming an ill-conceived alliance with a great army from the south…" and that, "as a consequence, they were removed from an exalted position and sent from beautiful Amia to Castle Marah, from which they were to govern the lands with difficulty the rest of their days…" Even with the little I knew, Grumwold's account clashed with what Kiran had shared with me the other evening. Which account was true? How much was Grumwold willing to do to protect my parents?

How ironic that another army from the south also plagued me. A notion started to bother me, like a sliver or tiny pebble, but I could not grasp what it was. I tired of trying to draw it out and wearily directed my mind elsewhere. Why did Abel have to irritate me so? I wished I hadn't left in a fury. He must despise me now. Why did it bother me to hear his questions about Kiran? Or about the son of the Mountain King?

I tiptoed to my balcony, shrouding myself in a wool shawl against night breezes. There, under the heavens, was freedom. If only I were a bird. This is what I experienced during those days with Abel and the sheep—freedom—but no. I shook my head as if to fling away the notion. Why did that man—he was short, unattractive, meddlesome—continue haunting me?

Because I care about him. The thought leapt unbidden into my mind. I exhaled slowly. Words lingered in the air before me, awaiting consideration. *I care about him.* I turned the idea over and over, searching my heart. *I care about him—about unattractive Abel.*

I admire him, perhaps more than anyone I have ever known.

I care about his good opinion of me.

I enjoy being with him. He overflows with contagious joy.

I feel safe with him, cared for as if he knew me better than anyone else.

I want to protect him from harm hanging over his head, and I don't know what I would do if something happened to him.

Oh dear.

This complicated everything.

But what about the son of the Mountain King? *I refuse to believe he's a hoax.* What about Kiran? His unbelievably handsome face and golden hair rose before my mind's eye. Kiran's knowledge, apparent great wealth and power, and tender passion for me made him an ideal choice for a husband. He was really a type of prince. He was also devoted to reinstating my birthright to make me not just a princess, but a powerful queen. Why was it that I didn't care about becoming queen when I was with Abel, but when Kiran was with me, it was all I desired? And what about the beautiful letters from the son of the Mountain King? I thought I knew his heart through them, even without meeting him in person. I had forgotten how filled with love his letters and his gifts were. But the effects of the terrible day and long ride had overtaxed my strength, and I staggered inside to bed. *I wish I could talk these things out with Hilda—I wish she were here—and Raven…*my mind drowned in sleep.

Bright daylight and Anna's soft rustling about the room hinted I had slept late. I stretched and yawned.

Anna slipped strong tea into my hands with a little laugh. "You'll need this, my lady, if you are to look even halfway alive for your special event at noon." She clapped her hands. "I'm just thrilled for you."

"Thank you, Anna, but—whatever for?" I took a careful sip.

"Why, your propos—I mean—your banquet should be fun. And it's a beautiful day." She flushed.

I raised my eyebrow. "Anna, how did you know about the proposal?"

Anna appeared very interested in dusting my desk on the other side of the room. "What proposal?"

I threw a pillow at her. "Who told you? Did Broden tell you? Did Kiran?"

Anna blocked the flying pillow and smiled mischievously. "A little bird told me."

"Little bird, my foot. More like a tall, bearded, redheaded bird."

Anna laughed. "My lady, Broden is Kiran's right-hand man, after all. And Broden only whispered to me because I'm his…well…" she stopped, blushing furiously.

I jumped up, barely catching my tea in time. "Anna, are you telling me that you and Broden are engaged to be married?"

Anna nodded, a smile breaking across her face. She bit her lip and hesitated. "I do hope you won't be angry with me, my lady, for not consulting you, but I was so sure you would approve of your favorite attendant–" she winked "—being joined with the head justice. What a position. And although most ladies would cease to work once married to such a prestigious person, that doesn't mean I will stop being your attendant, my lady. We already discussed this, and Broden agrees that I should continue in your service for as long as you will have me." Anna's words poured out, an overfilled river, as she finished fastening my dress. "And this makes me even more thrilled about your uniting with my own future husband's leader and friend."

"Just a moment, Anna—I never said that I was marrying Kiran." I gazed in the mirror. "Could you possibly pin up my hair the way Hilda used to do with my golden circlet?" I sat down.

Anna stared. "But, my lady. How could you even think of refusing?" She began brushing my hair with agitation. "What person in her right mind would not trade her right hand to marry the Enlightened One? And what a handsome man. He outshines all men, even my own beloved Broden, whom I just worship."

"He is quite handsome," I agreed, selecting an emerald comb that set off my dark hair. "His appearance is hard to resist, this is true."

"And his lovely manners, his great knowledge, his leadership, his devotion to you." Anna began to braid. "Let's not forget that he saved the kingdom. Really, my lady, I don't know what else a woman could wish for." She shifted her position and knelt before me, grasping my hands. "My lady, your marriage to the head councilor would bring the kingdom to a new era of power and prosperity. He is the wisest, most courageous, skillful man this kingdom has ever seen. With Kiran's magical arts, negotiation skills, and bold character, who knows how this kingdom would grow if he were in charge? Think of how you would increase the happiness of your people."

"Temptress." I laughed. "Stand up, you darling goose, and let me hug you in congratulations for your engagement. And now, please finish my hair, if you don't mind." I noted Anna's fiery eyes in the mirror. "You are a true patriot, Anna," I said thoughtfully.

"You know I was born in Marah, raised in this village, this kingdom. My grandfather perished in the Destruction, and my own parents gave their lives for this country. My family's blood flows in the rivers, sleeps in the dirt, blooms as flowers and thorns. I will be true to this land and to its advancement until the day I die. I love Broden, Hilda, you—but I will die for my country."

"Until now, my parents and I have done well for the kingdom."

"That is true."

"Which is why you and your own parents, I believe, have served so faithfully."

"Yes."

"Do you not believe that I am able to guide our kingdom well on my own?"

"Of course, my lady, you have always governed us well and wisely." Anna's face and the sharp edge to her voice betrayed her feelings. "And I am sure your wisdom will lead you to do what is best for your people," she added.

I wished Hilda and Raven were here. I examined the effect in the mirror and smiled at the results. "There. That will do for the banquet, I'm sure. You have done a marvelous job with this circlet. Hilda herself would be proud."

"You look beautiful, my lady. I'm sure I've never seen you look quite so beautiful." Anna finally smiled her approval. "Just exactly as a future bride ought to look."

I turned, taking Anna's hands seriously. I knew how important the kingdom's prosperity was to her. "Will you trust me, Anna, to choose what I believe is best? Will you trust me?"

Anna regarded me in silence and then slowly nodded. "I trust you to do what is best," she emphasized. Then she opened the door for me to leave.

CHAPTER 20

I paused by the towering double doors before the banquet room, drawing and releasing a slow breath until the doors opened by unseen hands to the sun.

I was dazzled.

Hundreds of flowers wove a rainbowed tapestry. Birds in gold cages sang melodies of heaven. Silver bowls of floating lilies spun the air with perfume. A huge table glittered like a kaleidoscope with gold and crystal. Mounded platters balanced the freshest and most succulent foods the kingdom had to offer. Wine sparkled in goblets. A roasted peacock covered with its flashing feathers formed the centerpiece. Milk-cooked goat, mushroom pastries, cream custard tarts, rose pudding—the dishes seemed endless. Kiran strode to my side, bowing to kiss my hand before leading to a cushioned place beside his at the table. "My queen," he whispered, tracing my chin. He raised his glass. "To the future."

"The future." I lowered my lashes and took a sip.

Servants stepped forward to fill my plate, and I exclaimed with delight over every dish presented. Finally, Kiran dismissed the servants from the room. The last one quietly closed the door as she exited.

"Now," Kiran said, putting down his wine glass

after we had eaten, "about the future. A proposal was put to you the other evening, my love, and I have yet to hear your response." He leaned close and gently touched the back of my hand with his finger. "I am ready to hear it now."

I avoided his eyes. Suddenly warm, I pulled off the shawl draped around my neck. Straightening my shoulders, I turned to face Kiran.

His eyebrow twitched.

I was not wearing the necklace he had given me. "Kiran," I started with a forced smile and then hesitated. "Kiran," I tried again, taking his hand, "you know how grateful I am for all that you have done for me personally and for the kingdom."

He fully raised his eyebrows and waited.

"You came in our hour of need, used your magnificent arts to cure my fever, and your wisdom to negotiate peace with our enemies. You even saved us from a possible rebellion from within, and you and your men faithfully serve the kingdom with all your hearts." I took a deep breath. "Thus, it is only with the greatest pain that I must refuse the highest honor and gift that you have offered me of your hand in marriage." I brushed away my tears. "For the pain that I know I must be causing, I can only say how sorry I am—I am so very, very sorry."

Kiran's face betrayed his shock. He reached out and caressed my face. "My queen, you do not know what you are saying. You have not yet rested enough after a trying day," he crooned. "Let us discuss this matter after you have rested." He pulled a small, golden harp from behind his chair and began to play a soothing tune while singing softly. The music was intoxicating.

I felt myself relax. Perhaps the Enlightened One was right after all. Perhaps this was the best way, and he was the love I had dreamed of all my life. Before I realized what was happening, I had closed my eyes and leaned toward Kiran.

He released the harp and reached out to kiss me.

The sudden silence broke the trance. "No." I jerked away. "I have considered most carefully to know my heart." My voice and resolve grew stronger. I held up my hand to stop Kiran's words, my eyes holding his for a long moment before I lowered my gaze. "I will not be persuaded to change my mind. I am sorry," I repeated.

Kiran's hand dropped. He looked at me coldly. "And what about the great sum that was taken from my personal treasury to buy your peace? I'm afraid it was not exactly a free gift for the taking." He raised an eyebrow as I flushed.

My mother had been right. Everything had a cost. "I—I will collect the funds needed to pay you back, every cent."

He laughed, his contempt obvious. "From taxing the farmers?"

"I will find a way." My mind raced. "Surely, a man of your great wisdom would see the benefit of receiving payments with interest over a number of years. You will add well to your treasury through this transaction. Let us set up an agreement with terms—"

"But why," Kiran interrupted, "are you set against me? Have I not done everything for you and more than you could have ever dreamed?"

"Yes," I said slowly, "but I have determined something that I had not realized I still wanted until last night. I will remain in my path of independence. I have ruled these years—as my parents before me—without the aid of anyone. I will not form an alliance with you, nor one with the Mountain King. I will rule, myself, as governor, and perhaps in time I shall prove myself worthy of taking my birthright as princess over the land." I forced a smile. I had always felt more confident in my role as a negotiator of peace than as a navigator of love. "I am especially grateful that because of the threatened invasion, I now see an area of weakness in my own kingdom and its borders. One that I am determined to soon remedy." A triumphant finish, and I paused for a breath.

Kiran had started to smile at me, which was disgruntling, and I was not at all certain that he would not break out in a laugh.

"Why do you smile?" I asked, a little angry.

"I smile," he returned with a sneer, "at your imagined independence. Surely, you cannot be so naïve as to believe you have reigned all these years without help and protection from outside?"

I stood. "I thank you, sir, for your time this afternoon. I must be going."

"Oh no, you're not."

My senses drowned in a wave of rage. Who was this impudent man? How dare he order me about, and in my own castle. Was this the same man who spoke love to me not a few minutes ago?

"Your insolence is intolerable. I am truly grateful now that I did not agree to your proposal of marriage. I am only surprised I did not see through your mask earlier."

"That's all a matter of perspective, Judah."

"What do you mean?"

Kiran pulled out my chair again and gestured for me to sit. "Join me for a few more minutes. What I have to say will be of great interest, I can assure you."

His smooth tone of voice caught me off guard, and I sat back down with a scowl.

"As I said," he continued, "it is all a matter of perspective. You see, when you refused my proposal of marriage moments ago, you thought you had all the facts laid out in front of you. That, however, is not the case."

"What are you saying?"

"I am saying that I am not only the Enlightened One. I am also the king of a great kingdom." He smiled as my eyes widened, and stood, strolling around the room, picking up items at random, examining them as he spoke. "As a king, I command a great army, one comprised of mighty warriors ready at my beck and call to do whatever I bid. I also, shall we say, have great power over the neighboring kingdoms of the south." He lifted a goblet to the light and regarded the wine's golden glow.

"How—" I began.

Kiran held up his hand. "You say you refuse my

hand in marriage. Well, it may interest you to know that when I left for that extended journey to negotiate peace with the southern invaders, I had a very easy time negotiating. Are you curious to know why?" He stopped to look in my eyes, a smile playing about his lips. "It was because the armies with which I negotiated were my own."

My ears grew warm as the truth began to dawn.

"Judah, I am the reigning king over all of the southern kingdoms." His voice became stern as iron. "The combined army which sat on the cusp of invading you, of crushing your kingdom entirely, is mine."

Kiran walked to where I sat, breathless, and plucked a blood-red apple from my plate. He took a bite. Juice sprayed my face. "So, you see, my lady, you just might want to reconsider your decision about the marriage proposal. My army is not actually far from your borders. One word from me…" He gave the table a menacing smack. I jumped.

Tossing the apple back onto my plate, he took a sip of wine before picking up my cup and offering it to me. "Well, Judah? What do you say now? Are you ready now to become a queen?"

I ignored the proffered glass, choking out the question I knew had to be asked. "If I were to accept your offer—what then?"

He laughed. "Why, then we would annex your lovely little kingdom to my own, and the two of us would reign together over the greatest kingdom the world has ever known. Who knows? Perhaps we might eventually oust the Mountain King himself."

"But why do you desire my small kingdom?"

"You have the natural resources that my own kingdoms lack. Together, we would have the strength to rule the world."

"And if I were to refuse?"

Kiran let my glass slip from his fingers to the ground where it shattered into a thousand pieces. "Your kingdom would fall, my lady."

"Your forces would attack?"

"And defeat, crushing all in their path without mercy."

"What about Raven? She is innocent? You knew this."

"Let us just say she proved a useful scapegoat."

"What have you done with her?"

Kiran sneered.

I shuddered. "Hilda? What have you done with Hilda?"

"She will return to you when circumstances are favorable."

I stood up shakily. "I—I will consider everything you have said."

Kiran took my hand and raised it to his lips. "You will give me your answer tomorrow by dusk."

I was not in a position to argue. I bowed my head. "Even so." I turned to leave but stopped to pull something out of my pocket, a small box made of stone. Placing it firmly on the table, I endeavored to speak without shaking. "This is yours."

Kiran lifted out the necklace, dangling it from his

finger like a chain. "It will look lovely on your neck again, my queen." He laughed.

I gave no answer and passed silently out of the room.

CHAPTER 21

I returned to my room and paced the floors that Anna continued to sweep around me. I plopped onto the couch and stood again.

Was it my imagination or was Anna on high alert?

"Anna, I'm going out for a while. Don't wait up for me," I said to her and waited for her reply.

None came.

I stared at my attendant for a moment. Something had changed. I sensed anger from Anna, but I didn't have time to chase down the cause.

I hurried to the stables.

Head Groom Brunter met me there as I took Adara from her stall. "If anyone is looking for her, please tell them that she has been led out to pasture." The truth.

I rode recklessly once past the castle. My heart drummed like winter rains, a deluge of anxiety, fear, shame. Adara, probably sensing my angst, matched with equal speed. How could I have been so blind to Kiran's treachery? How could I have imagined myself in love with such a tyrant? The road stretched endlessly. In my fear, I made a clumsy, easy target.

Finally, the break in the trees came into view ahead. Abel was reuniting a lamb with its mother when I burst from the forest edge, scattering sheep. I reined Adara and leaped from her. Running to Abel, I threw myself at his feet crying, my face to the ground as I spoke. "Raven—she is a servant of the Mountain King, isn't she?"

He sat down beside my prostrate figure and spoke gently. "Yes."

My guess had to be true, and I had no need to hesitate. "And you—you actually came with her from the courts of the Mountain King, didn't you?"

"Yes."

I looked up in anguish. "Then, if you are a servant of the Mountain King, have mercy on my kingdom, I pray, and entreat the Mountain King on my behalf."

"What has happened, Judah?" Abel's voice was a summer rain to my scorching agony.

"Kiran has deceived us, and I have nowhere else to turn." Fighting sobs, I recounted my conversation with Kiran.

"Why do you not seek the advice of the councilors?" he asked quietly when I finished.

"I feared they would all side with Kiran, and that I might be betrayed by my own. Kiran and his men have many allies in the kingdom now."

"Why do you come to me?"

I regarded him, pleading. "I thought—perhaps—I know that the army of the Mountain King is the greatest in all the world. I thought that if his servant was to send word, the Mountain King might send his army to defeat Kiran and save me—us—from a fate worse than death." Lowering my eyes, I whispered, "Perhaps, for the sake of my original betrothal to his son, the Mountain King would be willing to come."

Abel watched me with interest. "But why do you come to me? You know the people of the forest would take your request to the Mountain King. Why not ask them?"

"I—I—don't know." Tears coursed down my face. "All I knew after that terrible conversation was that you would be able to help me. So, I came." I wiped my swelling eyes. "I realized that if Kiran had been deceiving me all that time, everything evil he spoke concerning you and Raven must be the opposite of what he said, and you both must truly be servants of the Mountain King." I gasped, covering my mouth, eyes wide. "I behaved so horribly to you last night."

"All is forgiven." Abel hushed my sobs like a mother with her child.

"Is it too late?"

"It is not too late. The time is right. Come." He took my hand and led me to a rocky point overlooking a wide view of the lands below. "Look to the lands of the south."

I surveyed the area he indicated.

"All the armies that belong to Kiran will be annihilated by the Mountain King, and one day, Kiran himself will be destroyed, but first, there are other things that must come to pass."

My heart fell at the last statement, but I recovered.

"I will come with you now," Abel continued.

"And defeat Kiran?"

"Yes." Abel's face had a strange look that I could not decipher. "You will remember these things, Judah?

Even when all seems wrong, you will remember these things?"

I was surprised but answered. "Yes, I will remember."

"Come." He took my hand again and brought me to where Adara grazed. He tightened his lips and appeared as if sending a whistle, but I heard nothing.

Suddenly, galloping to Abel from the trees, there came a huge stallion. It was white as the pure peaks of the mountain itself, and it thundered as the Great River in the floods.

Abel smiled and rubbed the horse's nose, the most incredible animal I had ever seen, surpassing even beautiful Adara. I tentatively reached out my hand. When Abel nodded, I stroked the stallion's nose. Adara nudged me from behind. Jealous and shy, I judged, and I gave her a reassuring hug. Then I sputtered, "But—how did he hear that? I heard nothing."

Abel laughed. "There are some songs that are meant for all to hear, and there are some songs that are meant for only one to hear." He helped me mount Adara. "You have your own, you know."

"I almost forgot." My face flushed. "Thank you."

We sped to the castle, discussing many things. The sun was setting, and darkness had fallen when we arrived.

As we neared the village, I steered Adara to a path that would mostly protect us from any eyes casually looking in that direction. This path wound its way up and around until it connected with the secret gate at the back of the castle. We dismounted to walk the horses to the gate. I hesitated a moment, listening carefully. Beckoning for Abel to follow, I led the way through.

I pushed open the gate. Hooded men stood before us. Abel and I were gagged. A cloak was thrown over my head, and I was carried away.

CHAPTER 22

I didn't have time to think or scream. Struggling like a netted lion, I bit and slammed until the tightening gag and bonds and grips forced me to cease. But I heard not a sound from Abel. After my blindfold was whipped off, I blinked at the sudden light. Then my eyes adjusted. I gasped.

Abel stood beside me in the great hall facing the dais.

The room blazed with torches. Courtiers, faces filled with uncertainty, mixed with followers of Kiran around the hall.

Kiran stood on the dais.

A triumphant smile flickered across his face. He stalked down the steps toward us, the hunter and his prey. "What is this? The governor of the land, a lady of royal blood, has formed an alliance with a shepherd?" Kiran laughed. "How picturesque." He circled slowly. "You must truly be desperate, Judah, to have dug down this far."

I was about to reply but glanced at Abel first. He shook his head slightly in warning.

I remained silent.

"How interesting, though," Kiran continued, looking intently at me, "that the woman who declared herself independent earlier this very day, rushes out directly to ask for help." He paused, raising mocking eyebrows. "What do you have to say for yourself?"

"You agreed to wait until tomorrow at dusk," I replied, clenching my teeth. "How dare you assault my guest and me with your brutes?"

"Quite the guest," Kiran studied his hands, as if nothing mattered to him. "And quite an entrance. Why, one wonders, was the governor sneaking through a hidden back gate in the company of a shepherd? And not just any shepherd, but one who, by the way"—Kiran shifted his gaze to Abel, who did not react—"was recently identified as being connected with a condemned traitor."

Murmurs rustled through the crowd.

"I have called these people here tonight so they may know the truth," Kiran raised his voice. "Where does the loyalty of our governor actually lay? With this land or with the kingdoms of the south?"

"You lie. You are the traitor, Kiran." I turned to the people. "He is the one who is allied with the south. He is trying to force me to marry him so that he can gain control of our lands. This, we cannot let him do." I struggled with my bonds, but they held fast.

Kiran watched me with a tolerant smile but with an evil glint in his eyes.

"You must believe me. Have I not earned your trust, my people? Can you not see through this evil man's scheme?" I begged.

"Your people, my lady," Kiran replied, "are already aware of the lies you are prepared to speak to cover your foul deeds and the treacheries of your so-called chosen friends." He peered at Abel, but still, Abel said nothing.

My fury surged, a white fire. "I will never marry you, and what's more," I glanced at Abel, "we will defeat your armies completely—you have nothing to stand on."

Kiran had caught my look. He shifted his attention to Abel. "And who is this traitor, really? Who is this pretender who goes around in the guise of a man of the flocks?" He turned to the crowd, leveling his arm at Abel as he shouted. "Who is this man who plots with your governor to take control of the kingdom and turn it over to its enemies?" He spun back to Abel. "Do you not answer me?"

The hall remained dead silent.

Kiran stepped closer, his finger in Abel's face. "Are you the son of the Mountain King?"

I stared.

"You have said it," Abel answered in a soft, clear voice that echoed around the hall.

The echoes of his words slammed back, knocking breath from my lungs. The room spun.

I had worried Kiran might guess Abel's identity as a servant of the Mountain King, but this. I opened my mouth, but no words came. Raven had spoken truth that day. I had believed her to be ill, believed her to be mistaken, believed anything but the seemingly ludicrous words she said.

Abel faced Kiran.

Please turn. Please look at me. And yet I dreaded it.

My words, my deeds flew before me, a swift, dark flock crying my errors. Better if the earth swallowed me up, hiding me from Abel's face.

Kiran's eyes gleamed, a cat on the hunt. "This changes everything, of course," he began. "It does not matter what Judah has decided, nor what military forces you may have ordered to prepare for battle against my own, does it?"

"No," Abel replied.

"You are already aware of the terms?"

"Yes."

"Wait—" I tore through astonishment—where was my voice? —and avoided looking at Abel. "I don't understand. You want to marry me for my lands, and though I refuse, you say that our military force does not matter?"

Kiran shook his head with ill-disguised condescension. "Judah, Judah. I know you grasp that I do not desire to marry you for your own dear self, but you cannot truly believe I wanted to marry you only for your little kingdom?"

"I don't understand. That is what you told me earlier today."

"You darling thing. Your tiny kingdom is sweet, but it is not an end in itself. No, Judah, there are greater things here at stake than love or money or power."

I waited.

"Revenge, Judah, sweet, inexhaustible revenge, driven by the purest hatred known to the universe." Although he spoke to me, I was certain his words were intended to provoke Abel. Kiran's face twisted maniacally. "What I mean to say is this: You. Belong. To. Me." Each word dropped from his mouth like a stone.

"What do you mean?" Horror grew by the second, but I pushed forward, wielding words like a sword. "I belong to no one until I so choose. It is my birthright." I nodded toward Abel. "The son of the Mountain King can confirm that I was given the right to my own marriage destiny by the Mountain King himself in the days before I was even alive."

Abel turned and gazed at me then.

My heart almost broke under his look.

Meanwhile, Kiran had swept to the top of the dais. He reached into his robe, producing a scroll. This he untied, his voice ringing around the room in triumph. "Your birthright? Behold." He flourished the parchment for all to see, letters of gold gleaming in the torchlight.

I shuddered, gaping. What was that? Sorcery? How was that in his hands?

"I am the irreversible possessor of the betrothal document of Judah. She shall be my wife according to the law of the Mountain King himself, which can be undone by no one." The deep hatred of Kiran for the Mountain King and his son now shone plainly for all to see, a black, insatiable fire. He regarded Abel, obviously elated. The document in Kiran's hand stared at me accusingly.

It must be a dream, a nightmare.

"It cannot be—" My whisper grabbed with

spectral hand at tendrils of past certainty. Then again, in a voice swelled with disbelief and despair, I declared, "It cannot be." Impaired by bonds, I fumbled for the delicate chain holding the tiny gold key Grumwold had entrusted to me years before. "I have the document. It has been kept in secrecy and safety these many years. What you hold in your hands is a forgery." Finally, I managed to extract the key and thrust it as high as I could. "If you do not let me go and procure the document myself, I will shout to the world where it is hidden, and you will be proven false despite anything you might do to stop me."

"On the contrary, there is no need to shout. Bring the lady wherever she desires, and then return her here directly," Kiran coolly ordered two men. They cut the cords binding my hands and escorted me to my chamber where a gold box containing the betrothal was hidden in the wall. The men watched with interest as I removed the painting of Amia and lifted out the box. My fingers were clumsy with anxiety, and the clasp eluded me. I finally tore the delicate chain from my neck.

The key fit perfectly.

Everyone held their breath.

I raised the lid and snatched the scroll inside with a cry. This must be the betrothal document. I was safe. A quick tug broke the seal of the Mountain King. Black ink covered the page—words, smooth and elegant. At the top where the name of the scribe was recorded, letters jumped out to slap me in the face: *Mesda*.

My hands shook. How did that sister of

Grumwold manage to haunt me from the grave? I started reading. My heart sank. Something was amiss. This was not a betrothal document. What had the woman recorded under direction of the Mountain King himself, and how had it come to be placed in this most sacred box? The guards stirred uneasily as I read:

In a country of many rivers, a verdant valley wound through the foothills of the Great Mountain, becoming plains that stretched out to lands beyond. At the time of this story, the Mountain King built a palace in those foothills where he set a king and queen to rule the land. The palace was beautiful, filled with light and riches and glory surpassed only by the surrounding gardens. These gardens, crafted by the Mountain King himself, flourished with dazzling flowers, trees, and tamed animals. The palace was named Amia, meaning beloved, delightful. People may wonder if the beauty of this perfect place outshone the royal couple themselves, if they were truly worthy of the magnificence.

They were.

King Leo and Queen Elanna had beauty unmatched in the world, a beauty that shone both inside and out. For not only were they themselves beautiful, but they were also good. And they were not only good, but they were also wise. And they were not only wise, but they were also kind. The people of the land were happy for such a couple to rule over them, and they rejoiced at the royal coronation as in the glad years that followed. Villagers and farmers and shepherds cheered whenever they saw the good King Leo ride his great horse to visit the people of the land, where he gave advice or justice as needed. Queen Elanna frequently accompanied her husband on these expeditions. In contrast, she was as golden as her husband was dark, and her long, fair hair, which matched her noble steed, was as admired as was her sweet laughter and gracious ways. None in the land were esteemed as much as this king and queen, and none in the land deserved praise and gratitude more than they.

Shortly after the coronation the king and queen were summoned to the palace of the Mountain King, where they were greeted and treated as honored guests. Most people cannot describe the palace of the Mountain King, for most have never visited. When travelers who have been there are asked to tell of its beauty, tears of awe fill their eyes, and they stand silent. One can only speculate that the splendors of the palace are fit for the glory of the Mountain King, above imagination. King Leo and Queen Elanna's visit to the palace lasted some time, as it was planned for the purpose of creating a document. But not just any document.

This document, scripted in letters of gold on fine parchment and signed with the seal of the Mountain King, bound the daughter of King Leo and Queen Elanna in irrevocable betrothal to the bearer of the document. The king and queen did not have any children at this time, but the Mountain King knew that they would eventually have a daughter. When he communicated this to the couple along with his desire that their coming child would wed his son when the time was right, the king and queen were overwhelmed. They tried to convince the Mountain King to keep the sacred document in his own palace. But he would not. "Even the greatest gift," he told them, "is corrupted without love, and there is no true love without the freedom to choose." When the couple understood that they and their future daughter had been given the right to refuse or accept the gift of betrothal, their awe increased tenfold, and the journey back to their own home was silent with deep wonder.

Years flowed by, but the queen did not become pregnant. Although the king and queen and their court were happy and prosperous, time dimmed the awe of the visit to the Mountain King's palace, and a cloud of restlessness settled. Queen Elanna began taking long rides into the countryside alone. Although she shared the same cheerful grace with the people she met as before, they all noticed disquiet. One day during her ride she paused to rest under a tree and fell asleep. The queen was startled awake by the sound of a beautiful voice a short distance away singing a sorrowful tune. Soon, a dark-robed man of noble bearing walked into view, singing and leading a glossy black horse.

"Where are you going, honorable stranger?" asked the queen.

"I travel the wood, my lady, seeking to lessen the burdens of mankind," he replied.

"Your song stirs my heart strangely—I felt it long before I heard it, I think."

"I thank you. My only pleasure is that of being of service to those who need it most."

The queen, delighted by the singer and the song, invited the man to come with her to meet her husband. King Leo was equally impressed by him, and the king and queen whispered to each other that the man and his song struck a perfect chord with the restlessness in their hearts. Together, they urged the man to stay and live at Amia with the court. He graciously accepted.

More time passed, and the dark-robed man with the beautiful voice and courteous speech rose in honor until eventually he was placed as the head councilor to the king and queen. But change was slowly noticed in the kingdom. The other councilors began to be dismissed, and fewer courtiers were allowed daily into the throne room. The head councilor soon had an almost exclusive influence on the king and queen, and he began to put forth questions that they found difficult to answer:

"Do you really believe you have been placed in this position to remain in power?"

"As you are, can you not see you will never know the meaning of true power?"

"Do you really think the Mountain King has the best in mind for you? Can you not see that his jealousy will rise before long?"

These whispers in the council chamber echoed in the hearts of the couple long after each day ended.

Gradually, the king and queen began to keep more to their palace. They eventually stopped riding about the kingdom altogether. The previous sense of disquiet grew into palpable agitation, and the king and queen did not smile as they had before.

"The Mountain King has tricked you. You will be betrayed by him, and all will be lost." These words, first hinted privately by the head councilor in the ears of the royal couple, were eventually whispered in the halls of the palace. From there, the words spread to the villages and throughout the lands. Voices that had once risen in praise of the Mountain King were now raised in suspicion, then anger, then hate. The kingdom and its rulers grew ripe for that heavy, low-hanging fruit—war. When the head councilor suggested that an army be raised to attack the Mountain

King and take the absolute power over the lands for themselves, the king and queen silenced their hearts and agreed. Swift messengers were sent throughout the land, pleading for all ready for a new era of freedom to join ranks and conquer the Mountain King. But the shepherds were among the few that did not heed the call to rebellion. They gathered their flocks and left for a distant country. Notwithstanding, men and women prepared to fight.

Faces filled with hate, hands filled with weapons soon swelled the villages, but King Leo quickly saw as he rode among the army that there were not enough people for an attack.

But armies can be hired, and the head councilor knew of an army, large and powerful warriors, that might be engaged for such a battle. As long as the proposed terms were accepted. These terms were presented to the royal couple in private, terms more awful than they could have guessed. "How can we do such a thing?" gasped the king and queen. But by then the lust for power was deeply rooted in their hearts. They did not refuse the offer in disgust, choosing rather to justify making the decision they desired. Their hands trembled as they gave the document required as payment.

The king and queen left the council chamber that day, pale and troubled. But Queen Elanna persuaded herself and her husband that this was the only true and right course to take. A messenger left before nightfall to bring news of the payment to a dark army encamped beyond the plains.

But still, regret and fear surfaced which only seemed to dispel with music. At those times, the head councilor played and sang to the king and queen songs of triumph, bringing them reassurance, confidence. "We will not be overthrown. We will rise and prove ourselves equals to the Mountain King himself," the king and queen whispered when doubts rose in their minds.

By the week's end, trumpets heralded the advance of a massive combined army comprised of villagers and farmers and warriors, all with one goal directing their hearts and steps—rebellion against the power of the Mountain King. Together, King Leo and Queen Elanna led the army. As they marched, swords raised, armor flashing as jewels in the sunlight, banners whipping in the wind, people cheered from the walls and gardens of Amia and the countryside around. The head councilor rode behind the royal couple, singing a song of wisdom and glory and honor. The thunder of thousands marched across the land to the base of the Mountain King's home, and the shouts of warriors filled the skies.

Then a shocking sight stilled the voices. There, filling the plateau below the peaks, an army beyond measure was spread out waiting.

Silence reigned for what seemed like eternity.

Finally, a great man stepped out, glorious and dreadful in his might, the head of that silent army. The king and queen were terrified when they recognized the Mountain King, and waves of fear and shame overcame their hearts.

"Leo. Elanna."

They dismounted and hesitantly advanced to meet the majestic Mountain King, their heads lowered. In one movement, they flung their swords aside and dropped to the ground, faces covered.

"Why are you here?" His whisper pierced their hearts.

And then the Mountain King spoke in a great voice that shook the very mountains: "Why are you here?"

They could not answer the Mountain King. All wondered as he unclasped his glorious mantle, held it high for his own army to see, and then covered the prostrated couple at his feet.

Then he gave the command.

Not one member of the army that had come from Amia or the plains beyond survived the battle that day. The forces of the Mountain King swept like a flood across the valley, and all fell in their path. The King commanded Leo and Elanna to remain where they lay on the ground under his mantle. When he eventually grasped their hands to raise them up, the sight that first greeted them was his face, lacerated with tears. They turned and wept, for the horrifying destruction that started at their feet spread out to the ends of the valley, death blanketing the land as far as they could see.

"You cannot return to Amia."

The couple dropped sobbing to their knees at these words of the Mountain King. Their own hands removed the crowns still resting on their heads and the royal robes from their shoulders. A cry for mercy rose on their lips when the Mountain King's voice stopped their speech. "I still have a task for you."

Here the document ended. A soul-deep cry flew as a phantom from my throat. Why had my parents never told me? Had Grumwold known about this? She gave the key. Had she known what was inside the box and lied about it? Or had the betrothal been removed only recently? The parchment dropped from my fingers with dead leaf weight, signaling the nervous guards to guide me back to the hall.

Only a glance at my face was needed to confirm Kiran's claim. The sacred box, locked and protected from before the day of my birth did not contain the betrothal document. "But—but how did you come to be in possession of that document?" I cried out. "There is but one key to the box. How did you get that document?" I spat on the ground at his feet. "Thief."

Kiran tutted. "*Thief* is a strong word, Judah, one that you may not be prepared to back." Kiran waved the rolled document provokingly. "I did not steal the betrothal." He was obviously enjoying the moment immensely. "It was given to me."

"By whom?" My voice trembled, the words a jagged blade of the desperate.

"By your parents."

I gripped my heart. "You lie." I gasped.

"Not this time."

"Impossible." Suppressed sobs threatened to choke me.

"It's not only possible, but the verifiable truth, as I can show you."

But he didn't have to show me. I suddenly understood everything.

He nodded. "Ah, you comprehend. Perhaps there was something in that box, after all? A history parchment? Yes, it is in your eyes—you have read the history, and you know that what I say is true." Kiran sneered at my obvious misery. "You see, Judah, King Leo and Queen Elanna were desperate to hire forces necessary to defeat their supposed enemy—the Mountain King. They brought me into their strictest confidence. I proposed an advantageous deal, one that I knew would prove useful when the time was right."

"They gave you my betrothal in exchange for your army and then kept it a secret all these years? That was the cost described in the scroll?"

My world lay shattered around me, the broken pieces made of whitewashed clay instead of marble. But an incongruity dawned on me. "How were you even alive at that time?"

"My origin is not the same as your weak substance." He straightened and moved with swagger.

"But all were slaughtered outside of the rulers in the Destruction. Not a living being in the army remained."

Kiran smiled. "I managed to slip out before the battle started." He chuckled. "I think the Mountain King would have been a little more careful to ensure I was dead if he were able to see where his beloved son would end up today." He sneered at Abel and then continued, "I'm afraid, Judah, the reality is that you have never even had a choice. The choice was made for you before you were born. You have always been mine."

"But the son of the Mountain King—" I turned desperately to Abel. "You sent letters, gifts to your betrothed, to me." Wrenched with despair, I knelt at his feet and almost missed the word he whispered beneath his breath.

"Trust."

I lifted my face to meet his gaze. Tears like rain wet my cheeks, and—what was this? Tears also in Abel's eyes. I watched Abel's face and spoke to Kiran. "Where do we now stand?"

"It's time for a wedding." Kiran laughed. "Unless—"

But he had turned from me. He was talking to Abel.

CHAPTER 23

"Unless?" I whispered, a word suspended from a spider's thread.

Kiran suddenly pulled a knife from beneath his robe. Faster than the eye could follow he thrust his knife at Abel, slicing through the cords binding his hands.

I screamed, but Abel did not flinch. "If you are the son of the Mountain King," Kiran cried, "take this woman and flee. The people of the woods will hide you, and you will be safe. Run before my mercy is ended."

But Abel did not move. I staggered up to Abel in confusion. "Let us go," I urged. "Please." Why did he not move? "Please," I repeated, clutching his hands.

Kiran and Abel confronted each other, Abel's face like steel. "You know the law," he said quietly.

"I know the law," Kiran replied, "and so, apparently, do you." His eyes glinted, his trap set.

Kiran slowly placed his flashing blade before Abel. "If you will not run, then kill me." He grasped his robes to bare his chest, daring Abel to make a move.

Abel returned his forceful stare. "The time is not right for that."

My eyes flickered between the men. *I must save us*

all—Abel will do nothing to stop him, and we will die. There was not a moment to lose. With a wild cry, I caught up the blade and swung at Kiran. But my speed was no match for his, and his arm whipped out with a blow that knocked me to the ground, stunned. The knife shot across the floor by one of Kiran's men.

"I see my property will take work to tame, but she will cower shortly." Kiran flicked a gaze to me and back to Abel. "Unless, of course, you would like to save her from her fate, Abel. I am a reasonable man." He reached out his hand to Abel, smiling. "All you need to do is submit to me, become my servant, join my men, and I will not only give you this wench," he nudged me, fallen and bleeding, with his foot, "but I will also see to it that you receive a prominent position in my kingdom."

The crowd whispered at these words.

"Let bygones be bygones, and unite under a common flag, a common purpose. Serve me, and I will give you the world."

Kiran's men chanted, "Hear, hear. Unity for all. A brotherhood. A brotherhood." Others joined in with what became a roar of approval around the room.

I finally stood, shaky, as under trial and condemnation. Broden broke from the crowd, seized Abel's hand and mine, holding them high in the air with a loud voice above the crowd.

"Judah and Abel. Governors under King Kiran," Broden yelled.

The people shouted their support.

"King Kiran. King Kiran. The reign of three and

rule of one." Broden yelled again.

Kiran shrugged as if he had no desire but to obey the crowd. "The will of the people." He smiled.

Abel pulled his hand from Broden's with surprising ease. "I am the son of the Mountain King. I will not serve you, Kiran." His words ripped through the room like an earthquake.

The people fell silent, and Kiran's face darkened. A few boos hissed from the crowd. Kiran paced, tiger-like, around us. "I offer peace. I offer prosperity. I offer fulfillment of your dreams, and how do you respond?" He stopped, his face inches from Abel's. "I will ask you one. More. Time. Will you join me?" Kiran's eyes blazed. "Speak." Without warning, he punched Abel powerfully in the face. Bones crunched, and I screamed.

Two men grabbed me as I flung myself at Kiran. Forced to my knees, I sobbed, helpless. Blood trickled from Abel's mouth.

"Speak," Kiran demanded.

But Abel answered not a word.

"Then you know the alternative," Kiran spat. "You know the law. There is nothing else you can do if you wish to save this woman from her doom. She is mine," he yelled.

"I will do it," Abel replied quietly. "That is why I came."

Kiran stopped as one stunned. Then he turned his gaze to the crowd. He appeared smug as if a trap which he set was sprung, and the prey was greater than his wildest dreams. A slow leer snaked across his face. "Abel, you surprise me. I hardly expected you—even you—to agree to that."

A sense of dread crawled from Kiran's words, gnawing at my heart. I stood still, afraid, dismayed.

Kiran watched Abel, his hands twitching. Finally, he raised his hand for an oath. "Do you swear to fulfill this word, without deception or resistance?" The Enlightened One leaned closer.

"Kiran."

Kiran staggered at Abel's voice.

"You know with whom you speak, and you know what I have said." Abel seemed to grow until he towered and blazed with power. No one could look at him. Some fell down with fright. Even I was terrified and hid my face.

Kiran slowly stood and regained his composure. He gazed at Abel with what seemed a hint of fear and gave a hollow laugh. "Then," he croaked, "on to the terms." Kiran listed the requirements on his fingers as if transacting a normal business exchange. "One, the date: tomorrow, early afternoon—a public show. Two, the location: up in the foothills near the gates of Amia would be appropriate, don't you think? Three, the exchange: the young lady in question will receive her betrothal document within the hour of the execution. Four, the method: a scaffold, I believe…"

"Wait—" I could not remain in silence any longer, and I struggled to stand. "What scaffold? An execution? What is going on? Who is supposed to die? What are you talking about?"

"Well, of course, there isn't a scaffold yet," Kiran's

lip curled. He snapped his fingers, and two of his men left the room, "but it will easily be built in the next few hours. It will be ready in time, I can assure you."

"But why a scaffold?"

"My dear young Judah, your ignorance is truly appalling." Kiran glanced at me disdainfully. "There is only one way in which a contract of the sort I hold—" he brandished the betrothal document, "—can be broken, or given over to someone else, and that is through an exchange—a blood exchange."

"What do you mean?" I hardly recognized my own voice.

"The only thing Abel can give in exchange for your freedom—" Kiran smiled, "—is his life."

"No." The truth sucked my breath as it became clear. "No. This cannot be." I wailed, turning to Abel. "There must be another way. Tell me there is another way."

Abel shook his head, tears flowing down his cheeks. I searched his eyes, and for the first time, I understood the love that shone from those clear eyes was for me.

True, pure, powerful love.

A sob fractured the silence—my own. I fell to my knees, burying my face in my hands. "Is there no other payment? No mercy?" I whispered.

This time, Abel replied, "There is mercy, but not in that way. What you seek would not be true mercy, but only injustice." His voice was gentle and strong, authority blazing sunlike behind it.

"And the army of the Mountain King? They will

not come to save us?"

"The time is not right for that." Abel bent down to kiss the top of my head. "Remember," he whispered and stood again before Kiran. "I agree to all of the stated terms."

Kiran could not conceal his pleasure. At a nod, Kiran's men cleared the hall of people, most of whom seemed to have no idea of what had just transpired. Kiran's men nurtured the confusion, murmuring conflicting rumors and motives and possibilities for treachery. By the end, almost everyone had a vague idea that something sensational and interesting would happen on the morrow, and that its occurrence was a good thing for the kingdom.

Two of Kiran's men lifted me to my feet. Abel had already been taken away, so I yielded. They locked me up until it was time for Abel's execution.

The few remaining hours of night passed as slowly as a thousand nights. From the window, I watched each hour rise and fall. Stars flashed with unsurpassed glory. Most inhabitants of the kingdom slept that night, quiet, at peace, unaware of what was about to transpire.

CHAPTER 24

All nights are vulnerable to the moment when defeat by dawn is at hand. But this time, the pale whisper heralding a new day brought dread, not relief. I had not moved all night. My neck had turned to stone. That first hint of light blushing the horizon—did Abel see it? Had he kept vigil?

The sunrise, unaware of the horror it brought upon us that day, was magnificent, breathtaking in its glorious eruption of light and color and song. Beams shot across the valley, up the mountainsides, into the castle windows, rousing some from sleep and others from sleeplessness.

Where had his thoughts wandered that grim night?

How does one meet the morning before death?

I stumbled from my window seat, legs and arms numb, as the squeak of my door lock broke the hush of dawn. Anna stood there, her eyes red and puffy, carrying a tray of food and drink. This she placed before me. I tried to smile, but nothing could hide the circles I was sure darkened my own eyes. "Anna. What grace it is to see a friend. How did you manage to get in? You will not believe what happened last night, although by now you surely know something."

Anna released a death-like moan. She dropped to her knees, covering her face with her hands, and—between sobs—begged my forgiveness.

"Why, Anna, whatever have you done?" Confused, I stroked her curls, trying to calm her. "I am sure there is nothing to forgive."

"My lady—I—I am the one who betrayed you—" Anna choked. "I should have trusted you. I thought you were disloyal to the kingdom." Sobs wracked her frame. "I…I see now that I was deceived, and now someone innocent is going to die. I can't help but feel that he is innocent, and it is all my fault." Anna grabbed my hands, groaning, rocking in angst. "What should I do? What should I do?"

My mind reeled. Without thinking, I attempted to soothe the distraught girl. I lifted the porcelain cup, added honey, and offered it to Anna. "Calm yourself, sweet Anna. Here, drink this tea." She bowed her head as if in shame. "No, drink it. There. Wait a moment." I eased myself to the ground beside her so we were side-by-side, facing the door.

"I don't deserve kindness, my lady, not from you, nor from anyone else," Anna whispered, her eyes downcast as she used my own kerchief to wipe some of the tears from her cheeks. She put down the cup. "I am so, so sorry." She took a deep breath, blowing her nose on my kerchief. Her features twisted, scrunching as if to hold back tears. Finally, at my urging, Anna told me everything, how she had hidden in a secret room and heard everything until my refusal of marriage to Kiran, which she believed to be deadly to the country's peace and prosperity. How Broden had convinced Anna that her duty as a patriot lay in spying on her mistress. How she had followed me the previous night to discover that I was forming an alliance with Abel and then returned to report to Broden and Kiran, giving them time to prepare their ambush. How she had hidden herself in the back of the crowd during the confrontation in the great hall. How the truth of her mistress' innocence and her own treacherous actions dawned on her during the trial. How she could not sleep from the overwhelming crush of guilt.

"I may be a traitor, but I am not blind, my lady. Only a few minutes of that supposed trial had passed before your innocence and Kiran's treachery became clear, and I knew my own sin. I could not bear the weight of it. I sneaked away and only later learned from the cook about Abel's sentence of death and your imprisonment. What I don't understand," Anna grew angry, "is how no one else in the courtroom seemed to see Kiran's treachery. The people stood as if under a spell. Why was that? My lady?" she added when there was no reply.

I sat quietly, wrestling under the torrent of shock, anger, and pity for Anna. "I…I wondered that, myself," I murmured those calm words that belied an inner battle. Bitterness, self-pity, hatred, rage—the fruit hung heavy for picking. My past self would have gorged on such fruit. But the man waiting to die would not, and now my heart sought his.

I would choose the way of Abel.

I forgive Anna—despite everything, I forgive her. How

could that be? Relief, sweet relief from that crushing load lifted the weight off my soul.

"I wondered that," I repeated with more spirit. Forgiveness released my heart to soar despite the pain of the day's coming evil. "But we cannot underestimate Kiran's powers, Anna. All I can assume is that he somehow blinded their minds or darkened their understanding."

"Still…" Anna bowed her head. "So, my lady, you see, Abel's death and your own imprisonment are on my head, and mine alone." She wept. She turned her face away, desolately sobbing anew. Even in the sincerity of her sorrow, Anna's natural dramatic flair could not be suppressed. She made the perfect scene of misery, convulsively tearing at her hair and wailing, "Why did I have to be born? Why must I live to see the day an innocent man dies because of my blindness?"

"Anna, hush now. All is forgiven—do not condemn yourself further." I took my friend's hand. "Anna, look at me. You need to understand," I hesitated, "that Abel is dying, Anna, because—because of me."

At these words, Anna lifted her swollen face, eyes wide. "What do you mean?"

"He has chosen to save me from the death..." Tears coursed down my own face, and I struggled to control my trembling voice. "The death that would have been my life." I stopped. "My parents sold me to my enemy. I accepted his lying embraces. I am a fool." I covered my eyes. "Now Abel buys me back with his life."

"He chooses your life over his own?" Anna

whispered. "Broden would never have done that—the viper," she spat.

I looked at her in surprise. "It is over between you?" I asked.

"It is," Anna replied. "I, too, have been a fool. Last night I found Broden and threw my engagement ring at him. I told him I could never marry a man who served a wicked master, and that he had to choose between following Kiran or marrying me."

I raised my eyebrows.

Anna walked slowly to the window, reposing in the same place I had sat all night. She stared outside for a minute, her shoulders shaking from repressed sobs. Finally, she turned. "He took the ring instead of me."

I hurried to Anna's side, enveloping her in a hug. Anna wiped her eyes. Then she straightened. "Now, tell me, please, my lady, what is it that you command me to do? How can I even try to repay my—" she shuddered "—my treachery? I will do anything."

"One thing do I ask, Anna," I replied.

"Say it."

"Stay with me today, please," I whispered, turning back to the window. The sun sent a blood-red streak across the sky. "I—I believe I am going to be brought up the mountain for the…execution…"

A crow cried.

"Are you willing to come with me?"

Anna knelt again, seizing my hands, kissing them. "With all my heart, my lady. I shall not leave your side, whatever befalls." She appeared thoughtful, her voice dropping to a whisper. "My lady?"

"Speak, Anna. You have nothing to fear."

Anna's brow furrowed. "As much as I wish to remain here with you until the time comes for…for—" she blanched and hurried on "—until later, it occurs to me that I might best serve you by staying outside this chamber for now."

"Go on."

"If I go out in the castle and village, I can be your eyes and ears. I was told you were only to be imprisoned until after the—until later, and you will be freed to do as you wish this evening. It may be helpful for me to gather information on who has remained loyal to you, who you should trust and who may not be trustworthy."

I nodded. "I understand. It will be a great comfort to me knowing that you are out there, for the kingdom."

Anna smiled, standing to leave. "One more thing, my lady." Her voice was barely audible, and she glanced nervously at the door. "I heard you were only being held prisoner so as to not arrange a way for the other prisoner to escape. If you wish—"

I indicated she should continue.

"If you wish," Anna repeated, her eyes glittering with patriotic fervor, "I will do all in my power to help Abel to escape. Perhaps, if I enlist the aid of the shepherds and other loyal subjects, we may be able to break him out of his cell, and—"

I put a hand on her arm.

She stopped.

"Dear Anna, you offer to risk your life, and for this I thank you. But, somehow, I know Abel does not wish it." I closed my eyes. "Kiran himself offered a chance for us both to escape, and Abel would not take it. Surely, as the son of the Mountain King, he need only say the word and legions of his father's army would be available for him to command." I shook my head. "There is something I do not understand. Abel told me to trust, and all I can believe now is that, somehow, at the last minute, he will save himself."

Anna studied my face, tears brimming in her eyes. "Then—" Anna squeezed my hand, "—I will do what I can before I accompany you up the mountain." She added, bowing her head, "Be strong, my lady."

After the door locked, I lowered myself onto a chair until my face rested over my knees. I was shaking—I couldn't stop. *How must Abel feel right now? If I—who shall be released at day's end—am like this, what must he feel as he waits for his death?*

Finally, the hour came.

I had monitored the sun's path constantly, as if keeping track of the time could slow its passing. All too soon, the door was unlocked again to reveal a pale, anxious Anna with two of Kiran's men, ready to escort me on the long walk up the mountainside.

A large, silent crowd wound its way up the overgrown road to Amia. Public executions had never been allowed while Grumwold was head justice, so the foreign practice drew macabre curiosity. We proceeded slowly as the men guarding Abel at the head slashed at impeding brush. It was not until late in the afternoon when we arrived at the overrun, locked gates of Amia. The scaffold had been built on a rocky outcropping of a nearby knoll surrounded by a small meadow where the crowd gathered. The waning afternoon light glowed both beautiful and horrible in its intensity. Anna opted to walk alongside me. As the guards led us to a place a short distance from the base of the scaffold, she squeezed my hand.

I had fought my own battle on the road up the mountain. *Trust,* I reminded myself, *trust. I don't know how, but Abel will make a way.* I hadn't even protested when my request to make the ascent next to Abel was rejected, because my heart told me he would not die that day. *Trust. Wait. Watch.* I knew we would walk down the mountain together.

The view overlooking valleys and forests was stunning. On any other occasion, I would have reveled in delight at the vision. The Great River was visible, its slow-flowing waters sparkling like a stream of jewels. *How is all of nature so filled with beauty and joy this day?* I wiped my tear-filled eyes. *I don't remember ever seeing such light before.*

People not from the castle village or surrounding farms were scattered among the crowd. Was it possible that shepherds and forest guardians were here?

My heart leaped.

I glanced at Anna, who nodded. She must be entertaining the same thought. Could they be planning a rescue? Would they save him? I glanced about, desperate for a glimpse of Abel.

Then I heard it.

My song. The song Abel had taught me what felt like so long ago, the song no one else could hear but me. He was singing it now. I saw him then—bruised and bloody and broken—staggering up the crude stairs to the scaffold, singing to me, singing of love. He gazed out and locked eyes with me. He smiled through the blood.

Oh, how he loves me.

I stared into the eyes of the man who was about to die for me, and then I knew what lived so powerfully in my heart, my soul—I loved him, too.

I loved him.

And there he stood, abused by his jailers, abandoned it seemed even by his own father, paying for an offence perpetrated by my parents. Atoning for the woman he loved—me.

Could he see my love now? Would he read my heart in my face?

Abel, Abel—I love you—look at me one more time and know this.

I fought a rising panic. Wasn't he going to save himself? He wasn't really going to die, was he?

Say you love him—shout the fact to the world. Say it now, before it is too late. Why wouldn't my lips move? Why was I suddenly afraid?

I wanted to run, to hide. If I knew how to sing the song back—but I had only taken time to learn to hear and understand it, and now…now it was too late. I could not sing it. Fear held me in its iron tentacles. I was a statue.

As the executioner pronounced the reason for

death, a lawful exchange between Abel, the son of the Mountain King, and the holder of the betrothal contract for Lady Judah, daughter of Lord Leo and Lady Elanna, my hand found Anna's again and gripped it tightly. My face felt drained of blood, my knees like water.

Abel turned his face toward the palace of the Mountain King and cried out something that no one could understand. The setting sun flashed a glorious beam on the condemned man.

I closed my eyes so I would not see the end. I could hear the jeers and mocking voices of Kiran's men. There was a horrible sound, and Kiran and his men cheered.

"Turn away, my lady. It is finished," Anna whispered, guiding me with her arm. But before we could take a step, a great noise rent the stillness, and the ground shook dreadfully. Massive boulders cracked, spraying the crowd with shards of rock. A giant pine tore loose, falling with a moan, hitting the earth like a roar of thunder. The mountain shuddered as if horrified at what had just transpired. People screamed and fell to the ground, terrified. Anna and I clung to each other.

Then all was still again. My knees buckled. Anna's strong arm kept me up. Cautiously, people stood up, eyes wide. There had never been such an earthquake in the history of Marah. Everyone stared toward Amia, and I turned. The gates to Amia hung open, broken on their hinges, the huge locks and seal torn apart. Nervous whispers rippled through the crowd. What did this all mean?

Kiran, who had fallen near me, appeared uneasy. He jumped up and barked a few orders about burying the body nearby. As his men moved to comply, an unnatural darkness grew, covering the land before the sun neared the horizon. It was as if the sky itself drew a veil to hide what should not have been. The crowd cautiously made their way down the mountain as quickly as they were able in the fast-growing darkness.

I walked as in a trance, gripping Anna's arm. I was going to walk with Abel. Why didn't he save himself? Why…why…. The remainder of the journey was blank, dark to my mind. I vaguely sensed Anna help me prepare for bed in my own room.

In that fog, something had gotten into my hand: a document written in letters of gold. "My betrothal—how—" I stared at Anna, bewildered.

"Kiran handed it to you as you entered the castle." Anna led me to where a beautiful painting sat propped on the floor. Anna nodded toward the hole in the wall. "You chose quite the hiding place for the betrothal document, by the way—I had no idea."

I stopped at the painting. "My parents—" I murmured and then paused, still confused.

Anna must have understood my trouble and pulled out the golden box for me. "It would be best, perhaps, to lock this away again before going to sleep." She handed me the tiny key for the box. "I found this last night after the trial—on the floor here."

"Yes—of course. Thank you." I went through the motions of unlocking the box to secure the document and then replaced it in the wall hole. While Anna painstakingly lifted the frame back into place to cover it, I crawled into my bed where sleep—merciful sleep—could hold my sorrows for the night.

CHAPTER 25

The sun, reaching for its daily zenith, pulled me from a deep, dreamless sleep. Blinking in the light, I lay still. Where was I? What had happened?

Then I knew.

Wave after swelling wave rose, soared, crashed on my chest. Crushing grief pounded, dragged me scraping along the ground only to begin again. I gasped.

I had suffered the death of people I loved before—my parents, Grumwold. But this grief—this was different. Someone I loved—who didn't deserve to die—had given his life to purchase my freedom. And now, what roiled and undulated such a tempest of feelings in my chest? Guilt for my own wrongdoing and that of my parents? That was part of it. Gratitude? Yes, for a sacrifice beyond repayment. And, strangely, a sense of being deliberately forsaken. Abel hadn't saved himself at the last minute. He really did die. Why had he deceived me about the defeat of Kiran?

He did not deceive. The light of understanding dawned slowly in my exhausted mind. He had said that other things must first come to pass. *"Even when all seems wrong… remember."* And he said to trust. The key point grew clear. He never meant to save himself or immediately defeat Kiran. He meant for me to trust that the Mountain King himself would deal with Kiran…somehow, sometime. Even if after my lifetime.

"And I am supposed to…to live, daily bearing this sorrow and this…hope," I whispered. But how would I ever rise again from my bed, much less live under the weight of such grief?

However, despite a resolve to perish where I lay, I was compelled by a very real, intense sense of hunger. I had not been able to eat at all the previous day. I rang my bell.

Anna entered so quickly that it caught me by surprise.

"Why, you must have been right outside the door, Anna."

Anna blushed and fussed over me. "I was worried about you, my lady. I set a chair outside your room. How…how do you feel?"

"I know I will live, although I don't deserve to," I replied and then muttered, "But I feel right now like I could eat a horse."

"The house maid will bring up food directly, my lady, so let me help you dress." Anna rushed around, pulling out dresses and shoes and hairpins. She glanced at me and then added a necklace to the array.

I leaned back on my pillows to stare at the ceiling. "Anna, I loved him."

"I know." Anna's words were hushed, reverent.

"He was not beautiful, and yet, he was the most beautiful person I have ever met." Before I realized what was happening, words poured out of my overflowing heart.

Anna stopped and sat down next to me. This time she was the listener, patient and compassionate, as I spoke about Abel and the events of recent days. She eventually forced me to eat while I talked, and finally informed me that Kiran was preparing to leave.

"What, is he still here? That serpent." I sat up.

"Not for much longer, I believe." Anna cleared away the dishes.

I leaped up and began dressing with haste.

Anna assisted and put up my hair. I held my star diamond pendant to the light for a moment. It spun, an opalescent planet. I secured it around my neck, and Anna smiled, looking satisfied. I squared my shoulders, my lips tight. It was time to rid the kingdom of vipers.

A great noise in the front courtyard spoke of Kiran and his men preparing their horses for the journey. Coarse jesting filled the air.

"Kiran." I marched to him, followed closely by Anna. "Have you not left yet? How dare you remain any longer in my house. Depart immediately."

"Ah, there you are, Judah. What a pity you didn't sleep any longer," Kiran replied with nonchalance. "It appears you awoke in a foul mood."

"Leave, you fiend." I pointed to the gate. "There is nothing else for you here."

"So feisty. One of the few things I *almost* liked about you." Kiran leered. "But you really ought to be careful of letting that get the best of you, even when you —" his gaze raked over me "—aren't looking your best. And how high and mighty you act now that you have your precious document back."

"This is my home, and you no longer have any claim on it. Be gone, trespasser, before I call my guards."

Kiran laughed. "Why, that would be truly terrifying. Whatever shall I do?" He turned a dark look on me. "Be warned, Judah. I am not through with you. Do not push me past my patience."

I took a step back.

"Oh, you thought you were done with me, did you? No, my lady." He stretched out the words. "My goal was to destroy you or destroy him, but now that I've destroyed him," he smiled, "who's to keep me from destroying you, too?"

I gasped. "How dare you. How dare you threaten me, after all you have done?" I fought to control my rage.

Anna touched my hand lightly in warning, an anchor in this storm.

I gritted my teeth. "Why do you hate me? Why do you wish to destroy me?"

Kiran reined in his impatient horse. "It's very simple. You are the beloved of the son of the Mountain King. By destroying you, or marrying you, whatever you wish to call it, I enact revenge on my enemy." He shrugged. "You played so perfectly into my hands, too, but the end was better than I could have wished. Now, I feel that finishing you off after your true love is no longer able to save you would be perfect."

At these words, my reckless courage deflated into

unease. What could he do now? I would not put anything past Kiran.

Kiran turned his horse toward the gate. "For now, I am leaving, Judah, but only for my own country. You shall see my face again much sooner than you may wish."

"What do you mean?"

"I mean," he motioned to his men, "in two days' time, I will be waiting on the borders of your kingdom with my entire army. Unless you wish to surrender your land immediately, consider this fair warning."

"But that is contemptable, malicious. You cannot do that."

"Two days," Kiran called over his shoulder as he galloped through the gate and down the road, followed by all his men and those people from the castle and village who had chosen to throw their lot in with Kiran. Thundering hooves echoed.

I stood with Anna near the empty gateway until all was silent. Then we climbed the stairs to watch from the wall.

"What are we going to do?" I was tired, defeated. Dust clouded the horizon.

"I don't know," Anna whispered, her eyes wide.

The valley below sparkled, a reflection of tranquil paradise. Soft, sloping green hills curved with deepening afternoon shadows. The river made its easy way to the lower lands, the only constant in a world that seemed ever-changing, unpredictable, terrifying. The enemies were no longer within my home, but they were about to amass at our borders. Yet the sun continued on its daily route, the breeze was a soft, warm one I recognized, and scents from the nearby garden arose familiar and comforting. The serenity of it all felt almost irritating. How could we hover on a knife's edge while the rest of life marched on as every day? Where were the dark clouds of doom, the stormy weather, the shaking earth, and alarming winds? I would have found these more to my liking at this moment.

Somewhere in the village outside the gate, an infant cried, a few dogs picked up an argument they had left off. Smells of evening meal preparations began to waft up into the courtyard. A cup of tea would be soothing. And maybe a soft blanket. Oh, for little Jemimah at this moment. If only the lamb could nestle in my arms, warm, comforting. Yet it was right that Raven should have her now.

I gasped, and Anna jumped. "What is it, my lady?"

"Raven and Hilda. They were sent to the southern lands, which means that Kiran has them."

Anna paled. "What can we do?"

"I don't know." I kicked a pebble, pacing, furious at my own blindness. "I'm thinking." I finally dropped onto a stone bench. "It's possible he wants them as a bargaining tool. He surely realizes that we are somewhat prepared for invasion."

Anna's eyes grew wide, but she nodded grimly. "Perhaps we can rescue them?" Her face fell. "Except we have no idea where they are exactly, other than being somewhere in the southern kingdoms."

"I know someone who can help us with that," I replied, a thought occurring to me. "He just might have heard something from his contacts. It would be worth a try, anyway."

"I will go find this man, my lady."

"No, Anna. I need you here with me. But I thank you with my whole heart. I will send a messenger, and we will see what we can find out." I stood. The valley still glowed, but now the scene brought its usual sense of peace. "Meanwhile, I will gather what councilors I can still trust for preparation of war."

"I can help you with that, my lady," Anna said. "Broden"—she hissed out the name as if the very sound tainted her breath— "told me which of the councilors came to Kiran's side."

I closed my eyes. What a blessing to have my friend back. "Anna, you are invaluable to me. And I would like you to do something else for me."

"Anything, my lady."

"When it is time for the meeting later, join us in the war council chamber." I smiled at Anna's shocked, pleased look and then entered my own apartments. It was time for thinking. My earlier brave words for Anna's benefit masked deep concern. My army was as an army of ants in the face of Kiran and his forces. My own capacity to lead an army was untested, and I would be facing an experienced, formidable foe. *Abel, what would you have me do? If only you were here to advise me, to help me.*

A timid knock interrupted my pacing.

"Come in?"

A woman entered. She was vaguely familiar, a housemaid, maybe? One of Grumwold's former attendants? She didn't appear too much older than I was, and she seemed ill at ease.

"My lady," the woman curtsied. "I am very sorry to disturb you. I—I thought…" She trembled.

I indicated a chair. "Please, sit with me. What is your name? How may I help you?"

"I am called Jenna, my lady." She wrung a white handkerchief in her lap as if she twisted together a lifeline, her face the same shade as the fabric.

I impulsively leaned forward to take her hand. "Jenna. How nice to meet you. Do you work here in the castle? Your face is a little familiar to me."

Jenna visibly calmed. "That I do. I have worked here since I was a tiny thing, waiting on your own mother, bless her. And then waited on Lady Grumwold, bless her. And now I help with the scribe work and the records. I…I didn't want to make you angry and lose my place." Jenna sighed and shook her head. "I have kept it quiet all these years," she whispered, looking down to her hands. "I didn't even tell Lady Grumwold, bless her, although maybe I ought to have done." Tears welled. "I have never been good at speaking, I haven't, and maybe that is why I became a scribe. The writing is different. Words come different through a pen than through my mouth, they do." Jenna blushed. "I wasn't trying to eavesdrop, I wasn't. After I finished the cleaning, I always waited for another task, but I think they forgot I was there. I didn't know what to do. I was such a tiny little thing."

Jenna paused. "The sweet old lady Mesda, you remember her, my lady? I took to spending my evenings with her, you see, and she took to teaching me since she'd been a master scribe and all. She told me, 'Jenna, you write things like a story, and details will follow.' And I thought maybe I could tell you what I know, after all, if I tell you like it was a story. I was in the courtroom the other day," she added, "and when I heard all the kerfuffle about papers and your parents and secret boxes and such, I knew where my story fit, I did." Jenna twisted the kerchief anew.

My tired eyes had widened while I listened, and now my own hands trembled a little. "Tell me, please."

Jenna closed her eyes. Her voice changed, flowing now with the lyrical calm of a river. "Your mother and father stood in their bedroom. Lady Elanna held a gold box covered with designs. Lady Grumwold had just come and gone, delivering a parchment which Lord Leo had locked into the box without breaking the seal, as instructed. A painting of a palace sat propped on the floor beneath a hole in the wall. Your mother—she was so pale, gripping that box—said, 'Are you sure we are doing the right thing?' She was pregnant with you, you know," Jenna added, opening her eyes for a moment to look at me. Then she blushed and closed them again.

"Lord Leo said, 'We have no choice. I cannot face what we've done. I fear that if our act should become known I would either die immediately or lose my mind.'

"'I fear the same,' Lady Elanna said. 'If only there were some way to go back.'

"Your father appeared angry then," Jenna said, looking at me again. "Are you sure you want to hear the rest, my lady?"

I nodded. Now I was the one ill at ease.

"Lord Leo said, 'Do you truly believe we would have done differently? Can you not see that we would merely repeat the offense, and how brutal to know that I would have done it all again.'" Jenna's face tensed. "He said, 'I feel as if a rebellion lived in my heart that was at work even as I served my beloved Sovereign, and I often hate myself for it.' Then he did the most beautiful thing, my lady," Jenna said, tears forming below closed eyelids. "Your father kneeled before your mother and took her hands, saying, 'I am so sorry, my love.' It was like a fountain pouring on Lord Leo's head, it was, and he lifted his face under Lady Elanna's tears as if receiving a blessing or cleansing. Lady Elanna wiped her tears off his face with her long hair.

"'As am I,' she said, 'I am very, very sorry.'"

A stream of tears poured down my own face as Jenna told this part. She opened her eyes and glanced at me anxiously, stuttering that she was almost finished. I couldn't speak, so I waved for her to continue.

"You father said, 'There is no undoing the past. All will become known in time, but it must be after we are in our graves.' Together, they placed the box into the hole and covered it with the painting. Lady Elanna took a chain with a gold key from her neck and sent a servant to bring Lady Grumwold back. They gave her the key."

"I asked Lady Grumwold why your parents were so sad, and this is what she told me, bless her, if you want to hear." Jenna peeked and continued when I nodded. "She said, 'Ten years ago, the Mountain King had sent your parents with the surviving people from Amia to the land at the base of the mountains. The only people not exiled were shepherds, who were already gone. They had refused to take part in the rebellion and left the land long before the army's desolation. When the last person exited the gate of Amia, the entrance was locked and stamped with the seal of the Mountain King.' Then Lady Grumwold told me that the only road up to the palace of the Mountain King started at the steps of Amia, which was now barred and sealed. She said that the way to the palace of the Mountain King was blocked from all who desired to enter, and over time, the memory of Amia faded. The road from Marah to that perfect place grew over and was no more." Jenna opened her eyes.

"I hope I did the story justice, I do," Jenna whispered, watching my face. I brushed away my tears and tried to murmur thanks, but Jenna quietly rose and tiptoed out of the room, softly shutting the door. She must have known I needed to be alone. My thoughts swirled—facts and questions intermingling with answers, theories.

So Grumwold had not known my parents had traded my betrothal. They had given her the key after locking the box—she hadn't known there was but one document inside. Why? Why hadn't they told her? Shame had led them to act in fear. And why hadn't Grumwold examined the box's contents before giving the key to me? Why hadn't she told me about the written history? What purpose was there in this all? I groaned and massaged my temples. I rose to pace, but my feet dragged, and I stopped by my bed. Abel had not been surprised that Kiran had my betrothal. He must have known how my parents betrayed me before I was born, which means the Mountain King knew about the betrayal and the betrothal document. I sat, picking absently at a pillow. Grumwold was a servant of the Mountain King. She surely was working under his orders to do what she did, which means that for some reason, I was meant to not know about the betrayal, about the history until I knew the son of the Mountain King. Until I knew him and wanted him, chose him for himself. I almost staggered under this weight. This means the Mountain King knew all along that there had to be a confrontation between Abel and Kiran after my parents betrayed me. He knew that Abel had to die for me to be free from their transaction. He prepared so everything would come to this point. Grumwold's actions were part of his plan for saving me from a fate worse than death. Yet did death have to be the fate of the man I loved? Was there no other way?

Now further deaths faced me and my people. Kiran's imminent threat to conquer us seemed like a flood rising to drown us all. I lay down and pulled a pillow to my face. I was no better than my parents. I, too, was deceived by Kiran. Would I now have to watch my own people face death for my mistakes? Images of massacres raced through my mind. I started to sweat. Was death to be chosen over surrender to Kiran? I would most likely perish in battle, and Abel's death would be in vain. Kiran would win, after all.

I sat up. The pillow tumbled to the floor, unheeded. "I am an idiot. I know exactly what Abel would have me do." I leaped up. The meeting with the war council would not be for another hour. But now I felt an energy that I had not felt for a long time. I knew that my plan would work.

CHAPTER 26

The swirl of deep mourning brushed my ankles with steady rhythm. *Breathe. Prepare for the quiet, sullen stares, and you won't be unnerved by them.* I knew there would be seats that remained empty in my war council, for several members had chosen to side with Kiran. I was running late, so I forced my feet to speed up and my inside to slow down with deep breaths.

This will be a poor first session for Anna. I envisioned my friend plopping down in the midst of fog-like silence, fidgeting with her hands until she finally sat on them. The image made me smile, but that dropped to a frown when I turned the corner and saw the council room door ajar at the end of the long hall. As I stepped toward the door, the dead silence I'd anticipated of a moment before shattered as though a dike had been breached, so great was the flood of voices. I paused, unseen at the open door. The room shook with wild fury, a terror and hilarity to behold. My jaw dropped. Opinions, possibilities, positions, tactics, countermeasures, arguments—all slung back and forth like so many clumps of mud. Anna seemed stunned, probably aghast at the lack of dignity and ceremony that surely should have surrounded the formal war council. But Anna's was not of a reticent nature, and not many moments had passed before she slung arguments with the best of them.

Before I could contain myself, a loud laugh escaped from somewhere deep inside, echoing across the sloped chamber walls. I clapped a hand over my mouth. The sound cowed the entire room into silence. Councilors glanced at each other sheepishly across the great table. Everyone stared at my dark mourning veils, their faces ashamed. "What is going on?" I sternly demanded. "What is this? What has happened?"

Anna blushed. I overheard her whisper to the neighboring councilor, "You mean this is not the way things usually go in here?"

"Not exactly," he replied through the side of his mouth.

Anna stared at the table and attempted to look dignified.

An elder councilor coughed. "We, er, decided to begin the discussion before you arrived, my lady. There were many, *ahem,* things to discuss." He, too, seemed to be interested in studying the table.

I raised an eyebrow, but smiled. "Well, I suppose *I* am the one who must apologize for being inexcusably late. I'm afraid I do not even have a decent reason for the delay—the fact of the matter is, I sat down on my couch for a few minutes to rest, and I'm afraid I fell asleep." I must have appeared as embarrassed as I felt, for everyone smiled kindly. Taking my seat, I invited someone to summarize the main points they had discussed. A haphazard synopsis of the chaos was presented to me for consideration. I nodded my thanks.

"Well, councilors, may I, too, present a plan for deliberation?" Triumph tickled the corners of my mouth.

"Please speak, my lady," Anna urged and then quickly covered her mouth and blushed.

"Unless the council disagrees, I wish to pursue a course of action that I believe will work, a course of action that I should have taken a long time ago." My voice dropped. The entire room leaned in. A few people prepared to take notes.

Tension quivered in the air like a violin's penultimate note. "Go on," someone whispered.

"My councilors, some time ago we received a stranger into our midst who appeared old and insignificant. She was sent for a purpose which I did not take the time to discover, much to my shame now. Who knows what may have been different today had I heeded this person at that time?" I cleared my throat and continued, "Dear councilors, I believe our only chance lies in going back to the point where I chose to ignore the guidance and warnings given me. We must take the advice of that wise woman named Mesda, sister of our beloved Grumwold and servant of the Mountain King." I paused, flushing but determined to continue. "I confess to you my own stubbornness and pride, and I humbly ask for your forgiveness."

Silence. There were tears, nods. A few smiles lit the faces of the elderly councilors.

"Mesda died with this instruction on her lips, and

it is not too late to heed the words of the dead." I stood. My voice rang loud and true. "With your approval, we will fulfill what Mesda pled with me to do. We will send a messenger to the people of the forest—we will ask for the help of the Mountain King. His son promised that the day will come when the Mountain King defeats Kiran, and who knows if this may be the hour? We can do no less than petition for his help. Councilors, do you agree?"

Hearty cheers erupted at this speech. Then laughter, joyful pounding. Anna rushed over and hugged me. A messenger was promptly sent for and dispatched with a sealed message and admonitions to make all speed ringing in his ears.

A sense of anticipation gave wings to the castle inhabitants that evening. All the servants did their work in a good mood. A house maid jested pleasantly with a cook, an indulgence in which they had not partaken for several weeks. The grooms sneaked extra carrots to the stables and stood around gossiping, bantering as before. The chief laundress even condescended to a game of cards with the lower house servants. Almost everyone had an excellent day and still better rest that night, with the exception of the head cook, whose mood and sleep never improved anyway because she suffered from pain in her bunions.

I woke before dawn the following morning. Anna had begged me to not hold the traditional nightlong vigil in honor of the dead, insisting I would need all my strength in the coming days. I agreed only on the condition that I honor Abel in my own way. Now, I dressed in the dark and threw on my shawl, anxious to be alone. There was something I had been aching to do, but the pressing matters of the previous day had prevented until now. Slipping out the back door, I collected an armful of the most vibrant, fragrant flowers from the garden and Adara from the stables. Shortly after, a kaleidoscope of color leading a golden horse crossed the gray meadows toward the path up the mountain.

I made my way up the road as a funerary procession of one, deliberately taking my time, letting my tears fall. Each step throbbed with the stabbing of grief. I fought against yesterday's events teasing at my mind: The messenger had returned with news that the people of the forest would bring the petition directly to the Mountain King himself. A reply could be expected later today.

But there were enough hours meanwhile for two visits: one to where my beloved died up on the mountain and the other where he had lived in the valley. This was the time for my burning sorrow. This was the time for remembering his love.

The air was still crisp from the recent parting of night. My black mourning skirts soon dragged with dew. Adara gently kept pace with me. I walked slowly, blessing the sun as it gradually rose to warm my shoulders. I had once wished myself a bird to watch such ceremony from above, but now my heart was too heavy to contemplate flight.

The road, mostly overgrown only a few days before, now lay trampled and easy to traverse after the crowds had marched that way for a deadly task. I noted with irony Kiran's men had cleared the way for the army of the Mountain King to pass on their way down the mountain.

I stopped among the white birches and evergreen trees. Almost there. The longing to see where my beloved died now tore fiercely against a dread of facing the site. Raw, shuddering breaths nearly choked me. My muscles tensed until I believed I would either turn to stone or flee. *I must do this.* Adara's reins dropped from my hands.

Just ahead was the place where Abel had died near the broken gates of Amia.

An upwelling surged from a deep, broken place. I wept unabashedly. Gathering the blossoms into one arm, I flung back the filmy black veil pinned to my head, a solitary mourner exposing face and loose hair to the sun. "Please, please know that I loved you," I whispered.

It was time to cleanse that defiled place with my love offering. I climbed the scaffold steps.

Two vials lay in my pocket. The first, pure water drawn from the Great River. I uncorked the vial and sprinkled the water over the scaffold floor. Water mingled with tears. The second, which released a pungent odor, I poured out carefully, strategically covering key points in the scaffold structure. At the place where Abel had stood, I gently lay the flowers. Silence. I rose. Nearby, fresh dirt piled high next to what appeared to be a deep pit caught my eye from that vantage point.

Shrugging, I returned to the ground and glanced at the horizon. I would have to hurry to have enough time for the other place. Quickly collecting dry twigs and small branches, I snapped and piled them at the scaffold steps, dripping the final trickle of the second vial onto the mound. Glancing around to note where Adara watched nearby, I withdrew the final tool from my pocket.

A flint.

By the time Adara and I were halfway down the mountain tearing at our frenzied pace, the blaze had reached the height of treetops. When we neared the forest's edge, a dying column of smoke gave the only hint of what had transpired. If I had been a bird, I would have perched on a stately birch on the mountain at that moment, gratified that nothing remained where the scaffold had been but a charred patch of earth near broken gates.

As always, riding Adara cleared my mind, and by the time we slowed for low-hanging branches of deep woods, my heart reached for memories. Jemimah, resting wrapped in my cloak as I rode to the shepherds. Hilda, riding alongside me, sharing our thoughts and company. Finally, there, the place where Abel saved me from the bear.

Then we broke through the tree line. Ahead lay the narrow valley where I first became Abel's friend. My other destination for today.

Dismounting, I led Adara to a small stream and let her graze freely. I wandered the valley, exhausted, empty, absently collecting wildflowers. I would leave a final bouquet here. As the morning warmed, I settled on a flat boulder and drew off my shawl. My hand went to my neck. I was sure I'd worn my star diamond that morning. Then I gasped, scattering the flowers, crying out at the realization.

I had worn my necklace.

It was gone. It must have come loose and fallen off during my ride.

My wail echoed around the mountainside. I had nothing left to give. I collapsed, tearing off my veil, clutching my hair, my face pressed into the damp moss. Why this new disaster? Hadn't I suffered enough? Now the last gift from Abel was gone forever. "Why?" I wept aloud. "Why this?"

A sound of a twig snapping tore the silent air.

I leaped up. "Who is there?" I didn't have even my bow with me, much less a sword. I stepped forward. "Show yourself." The silence that answered stabbed my heart. I sank back down. It must have been a deer.

That was when I heard the song.

Now, the beautiful sound was unmistakable. The song that only I could hear. I rose slowly. But that was impossible—Abel was the only one who knew the song. "I must be going mad," I whispered. What blissful madness, though—what glories resided in dreams and visions.

But now footsteps swept near. I watched the path from the trees with wonder. When a being came into view, I could not believe what I saw. A man, tall and glorious and beautiful walked toward me, singing. A dazzling smile surged across his face. His eyes were filled with love.

I rose slowly. Why did the man seem familiar? "Who—who are you?" I finally gasped as he stopped in front of me, "How do you know that song?"

"I am the one who gave you a promise." The man held out my star diamond, blazing white fire. "Do you not know me, Judah?" The voice, that gentle voice, was more beautiful than anything in the world. Bright, kind eyes, the look of love—he stood before me, alive. So very, very alive.

"Abel?" I whispered. "Is it you?" Then I threw myself toward him, sobbing and clinging to him as if he would disappear were I to let go. "Are you—a vision?" I quivered. "Please don't leave me."

"It is I, and I am real. I am alive." He softly moved my hair back. "I will not leave you."

"But…but…they killed you. Kiran put you to death. You were dead, Abel—I saw it. You were buried. How can this be?"

Abel—transformed, yet somehow the same—threw back his head and laughed and laughed, until the mountains rang with laughter of massive waterfalls, the crash of ocean waves, a windstorm through the trees.

"That hole…is an empty grave," I whispered. A smile dawned on my face. "A miracle."

Abel's eyes twinkled. "Yes. A miracle." He pounded the ground with his foot and gave a mighty shout that echoed down the valley. "The Mountain King set a law of life deeper and stronger than the law of death. Saving you through my death opened the doors of that law—the grave could not keep me. Kiran did not know that this death could not hold the son of the Mountain King." There was great gladness in his voice, the song of victory and life and light. "But he will know soon."

CHAPTER 27

By noon, the message came from the Mountain King.

I had been blessed with an extra set of eyes and ears all my life through the entertaining accounts of my dear attendants, my friends. When I returned from my long ride, Anna recounted to me the following events.

Everyone recognized the Mountain King's messenger—he had once come with Raven, bearing the final gift from the palace. The request for help had not been kept secret, so the entire village and castle acted as self-appointed watchmen. Eyes on the road from the mountain, runners ready to dash the news to the governor. Finally, when the sun had almost reached its pinnacle, a galloping horse appeared in a distant bend. By the time the rider had crossed the river, scores of youths raced to the castle gates. "A messenger. A messenger." The shouts rang through the halls as the senior councilor scurried over to the chaos.

"One at a time. One at a time. You—young lady—you are the tallest. Speak." Eventually, the elderly man managed to make sense of the cacophony, and by the time the messenger was admitted, a great throng of eager people followed. Most of the other councilors had assembled to greet him.

Moments after the giddy councilors invited the messenger to sit and refresh himself with food and drink, they urged him to deliver his message. Putting his fork down with a patient smile, the man stood.

"My friends, rejoice and be glad—the Mountain King sends his aid."

The cheers, laughter, backslapping, hugging, happy tears, congratulating at this pronouncement made it clear the message was life, hope. The messenger laughed with the loudest of them. When the noise began abating, he waved for silence and explained the Mountain King was sending a mighty army. They would descend to join the kingdom's forces by late afternoon. That would leave one day for the entire army to ride across the kingdom to the southern borders in time for the appointed confrontation. Satisfied that his task was complete, the man sat back down and dug happily into the food and drink that lay waiting before him.

Anna had directed that no one disturb me, leaving me to sleep and recover as she supposed. But she finally sent a servant to wake and bring me. Everyone had noticed by then that I was sleeping in strangely late. What a shock when the servant returned with news that I was nowhere to be found. The uproar was immediate. Every able body was dispatched to search the castle and its grounds. Then a mad rushing about the village, people calling my name, searching in impossible places such as under rocks and up trees.

Thus, upon my return, the scene which greeted my eyes was strangely similar to the previous evening's war council: namely, chaos. It took more than a few minutes for people to realize the governor was home again, and I had only gone out for a long ride. I endured several rounds of scolding, three cups of tea with scones from a relieved head cook, and relieved hugs from a worried Anna. At least six different people told me the messenger's news, but the story became so mixed up that I finally requested my chief councilors come and clarify what was happening. Then I gave orders for the kingdom's military to assemble with all haste. Messengers immediately rode out to the surrounding countryside.

There was no time to stop and consider the day's marvels as we polished armor, sharpened weaponry, checked horses, and supervised food provisions. Through all the bustle, a song filled my heart: *Abel is alive. Abel is alive.* Now and again, I pinched myself, ensuring this was no dream. *Abel is alive.* After time spent talking, walking with Abel on the mountain—infinitely sweet, filled with wonder—Abel left to prepare his army. He would return late that afternoon, but it seemed an eternity.

"You seem back in spirits, my lady," Anna noted.

I waltzed through my apartments, singing while changing clothes. Her jaw dropped farther when I pulled out an intricately carved box from the back of my wardrobe. I lifted the glowing robe inside, leaving my veil of mourning neatly folded on the bed. "You are feeling better?" she finally stammered.

"Anna, I am a new woman," I proclaimed, turning for Anna to help me dress. "I feel ready for anything."

"I wondered when you would finally wear this beautiful piece. In fact, I had almost forgotten about it."

"The time is right."

"I am glad for it," Anna said. "I believe I know what has made you feel ready for anything. It is the news from the Mountain King, is it not? Your hope has been restored."

I smiled. "Yes, but I have news that is even better. No, don't pester me to tell yet, dear Anna, I will share all in the council room soon. Now, would you mind doing my hair with that clever method you developed? You know exactly what to do with these curls." And that's all I would say on the matter. Anna had to be content with raising her hands in exasperation, scolding me as a tease, and threatening with the hairbrush.

Shortly before the expected arrival of the Mountain King's army, I met with my councilors one more time in the council chamber. The room shimmered as I entered wearing my incredible robe. I walked as a queen—not because of who I was, but because of the gift of the King's son. Everyone stared, their eyes reflecting the shining robe. I felt life in me again. But little prepared were they for my news.

And little prepared was I for their reaction.

"Councilors, friends, I have astounding news to share with you, news I can hardly believe myself. I do not know the best way to say this, so I will say it bluntly: Abel is alive. He lives. I spoke with him myself this morning. He is going to lead the army of the Mountain King to battle. He will return here to these gates within the hour." I beamed. "Isn't that the most marvelous thing you have ever heard in your life?"

Dead silence greeted my enthusiastic news.

People glanced at each other. Even Anna seemed panicked, staring at me as if she wanted to remove me from the situation without further embarrassment.

I sat in the ensuing silence. I leveled my gaze at everyone present.

They blinked rapidly and fidgeted, clearly worried.

Anna avoided eye contact entirely.

"Well?" I prompted. "Aren't you all just as glad as can be?"

A few people nudged a mousy-faced councilor who was known for her tact.

She glared at them. But they meaningfully winked and nodded as if her hour had come. The woman coughed discreetly. "Ahem," she tried.

I regarded her. What on earth was she going to say? This was not going at all as I had expected.

She coughed again. "Well, my lady, we are, of course, pleased that you are feeling so, well, inspired." Everyone nodded encouragingly. "And naturally, we, too, have high hopes for the imminent campaign." The woman was worth her weight in gold. "But we worry, my lady, about your health after the great strain put upon you over the last days. In fact, we all believe you would benefit from a decent respite before the campaign, if, truly, you need go at all, especially to cure any lingering illness."

Everyone turned to look at me.

They smiled, obviously hopeful that I would follow the polite suggestion without any more awkwardness.

I stared, unsure whether to laugh or cry. "You don't believe me." I stood. "You think I am making this all up."

"It's not that we don't believe you, my lady," a councilor said. "It's just that we feel you may be confused."

"Or tired," another said.

"Seeing things," a third person chimed.

My smile wavered. Now that I knew something worth believing, no one believed me. Abel had spoken of many matters that morning. How he had left the palace of the Mountain King at night for the purpose of winning me from the enemy who held me—unsuspectingly and obliviously—captive. How he became a shepherd, bringing back the shepherds and flocks after long absence. How over the years he had loved me, waited for me, had longed for me to return his love with more than the stiff formality that accompanied a promise from birth. He had told me all this and so much more. I held a wealth of knowledge from someone who had died and was now alive. Yet here I stood with no other way to prove he was alive than the joy in my own heart.

"Well," I said, "in that case, I suppose you will just have to see for yourselves."

People glanced at each other uneasily.

"What is she going to do?" someone whispered.

But that very moment, a servant knocked

officiously at the door. Upon entering, she solemnly announced that a gloriously large army was coming down the mountain, if the councilors would be interested in observing the spectacle from the upper balconies. The dignified announcement drowned in an undignified exodus from the chamber to see this historic event.

A distant rumble hammered from the mountain road. I stood on my tiptoes for a clearer view. It seemed every person in the castle and village strained to see them. Those who had ladders even peeped over the walls.

It was a truly marvelous sight.

Column upon column of warriors, clad in armor shining like diamonds under giant banners of blue and white, riding magnificent, pure white battle steeds. The army stretched back forever, a formidable, dazzling river. It was almost painful to witness in its brilliance. At the head rode a tall warrior who appeared every bit king over all the kings of the world. He rode with glad pace, his head bare.

Joy and pride welled in my chest. In my heart, I flew to him. If only wings would bring me closer now. The sight of this warrior drew exclamations, whispered conversations, speculations.

Then something else pulled the crowd's attention: a great movement along the edge of the woods. Silently, slowly, the forest rim lined with row upon row of innumerable people in dark green cloaks.

The people of the forest had come to assist the son of the Mountain King.

They advanced, rows of green soaring across the field to the road. The noble procession of white and blue met green, and once joined together, made way to the gates of the castle and stopped.

I had rushed to the main gates and stood waiting for them, for *him*. Gold embroidery on my robe undulated, flashing sunlight like the Great River in spring. The inhabitants of Marah gathered flowing around and behind me. I bowed low, as did my people, and cried out, "Welcome, Abel, son of the Mountain King. We are grateful you have come."

Shocked murmurs rippled around me, my words a stone thrown in water. Then a rising tide of elated shouts as people looked up and recognized Abel.

I stood, flinging out my arms. "You and all yours are most welcome, and we, your servants, are glad—glad—glad."

CHAPTER 28

The spy I had sent to seek news of Hilda and Raven met us on the road to the southern border. Amazement and wonder was evident in his wide-eyed gaze as he surveyed the magnificent company. He glanced pointedly at the crown on my head and bowed. He confirmed that another imposing army also made its way to the borderlands from the southern kingdoms, giant columns snaking through the marshlands and desert plains dominating those countries. Spears and swords met sunlight, he said, shooting bolts as if lightning terrorized the grasslands.

He also confirmed that Raven and Hilda rode with that army, clearly there against their will. Bedraggled, but alive.

"Your Majesty, Your Highness, the women held their heads high, but the one called Hilda seemed decidedly miserable. I'm not one to exaggerate, but I believe anyone observing the men and women making up those ranks would shudder under the malevolence in their eyes. They appeared eager to crush anything weak in their path. I thought to myself that the love of evil must flow like blood through their veins, brutality bulging in their muscles, vice sticking like tar, cruelty spewing as bile from their lips. It was no wonder the one called Hilda seemed miserable, for it was surely her first encounter with such complete, open wickedness. She clutched a little white beast in her arms as though protecting it from exposure to evil."

Abel and I exchanged glances. *Jemimah must still be alive, then.*

The spy grunted and continued, "But more terrifying, I think, was the evil probably hidden beneath a pleasant countenance, like flowers planted over piles of bones. At the head of this vile army rode an elite crowd of men who behaved differently from those in the columns behind. Rowdy and loud, these men laughed and joked with each other in a crass, familiar manner instead of marching or riding quietly in time with the others. Their chief, though, did not partake of their jocularity. His face was handsome and cold, his eyes steel. He rode as one born to lead. The people called him the Enlightened One."

He shared a few other details, and then, thanking the spy, we rode on. As we drew close to the designated place of meeting, we sent out a scout for additional information. A messenger was dispatched with a letter for Kiran, as well.

When the scout returned, his face was serious. "It was chaotic at first, Your Majesty, Your Highness. But when Kiran and his generals finished arranging the massive army, he gave his deadly directions: wait for the signal and then attack. Destroy everything. No mercy."

He glanced down. "The ladies Raven and Hilda were commanded to dismount and stand near their horses, their hands tied. They appeared exhausted. In fact, everyone in the army seemed weary after a time. I could see sweat pouring down necks, probably making shoes slippery—more than one person slid, and jerked, struggling to maintain balance. Horse dung turned the air putrid. Flies were everywhere.

"Then a single horse and rider appeared on the horizon, galloping with all speed, her battle messenger flag flying high." The scout paused, his face glowing. I smiled at his obvious admiration. "When she drew near," he continued, "the messenger reined her horse, dismounted, and ran to Kiran with a sealed note."

"What did Kiran do when he read it?" I prompted.

The scout's eyebrows raised. "Kiran laughed, saying, 'Is this a joke?' He threw the paper on the ground and spat on it, then said, 'This is all your mighty leader has to say to me? *Surrender*'?" The scout frowned. "He mocked you, my lady. He called to his men, 'Judah demands my surrender with a final warning that not a person of my army will be left unless I do as instructed. Ha. An army of farmers with pitchforks. This is a joke. How dare she insult me.' Then," the scout's face reddened, and he clenched his fists. "Kiran leaned forward and slapped the messenger, leaving a scarlet mark on her cheek. But she didn't flinch, though Kiran's men whooped. 'That is the message to give your leader,' Kiran said, 'I will never surrender, and she can burn.'" The scout glanced at me apologetically. "I am sorry, Your Highness. The messenger should be along soon—my horse is faster than hers, and I passed her a while ago."

Sure enough, the messenger arrived shortly after, her cheek still red from Kiran's slap. She quickly confirmed what the scout had said and added, "I saw Raven and Hilda. They seemed ready to collapse. But a great eagle appeared, uttering a shrill cry as it soared overhead, drawing their eyes to the heavens. The women appeared encouraged by this good omen. Someone in the crowd shot at it, but the arrow dropped harmlessly to the ground." The messenger bowed after receiving our thanks and then rode alongside the scout to rejoin the ranks.

It was time.

If I had been a bird that day, I would have perched on the mighty beech tree that marked the border of this country and the next, wondering as the earth began to tremble and shake with regular cadence, the air booming, reverberating, echo crashing into echo until my heart pounded. I would watch as, like the burst of dawn, over the hill rode what appeared to be a king and his queen, swords raised high, the cry of battle on their lips, sunlight flashing their armor with a blinding dazzle, riding beneath great banners of blue and white.

But I was not a bird, and I knew why the earth shook and the air rang. Behind us roared the mightiest army ever seen on this earth.

As we crested the final small knoll and stopped, Kiran rode forward on the other side of the field, halting in front of his grim forces, his face an emotionless mask.

"Kiran." The powerful voice of the man beside me commanded the attention of all. "Why are you here?"

"I have an agreement with Lady Judah to meet here at this hour on the field of battle," Kiran growled. "Pray, who are you, and where is Judah?" He added with a sneer, "Or has she hired out her dirty work like her parents before her? Perhaps she is too afraid to meet me herself."

"I am here," I called out. "I have kept the agreement."

Kiran's eyebrows rose, and he shielded his eyes. "Ah, Lady Judah, a crown and such shining armor. I didn't recognize you. Who is your friend? He has no right to be here with his army for our meeting."

"You know who I am," Abel replied. He rode forward, a veritable column of fire in the late afternoon light. "As the betrothed of the Princess Judah and as the son of the Mountain King, I have the right to be here."

Kiran staggered back. His face drained of color. "Abel?" he whispered. "How? You were dead."

"Why are you here?" Abel's voice shook the hills.

Kiran recovered himself. He raised his sword high, his voice loud and terrible. "I am here because I, the Enlightened One, will ascend. I will sit enthroned as king over all, my throne rising above the clouds and the stars. I will be greater than the Mountain King himself." He shrieked. "You shall not stop me. Betake yourself and your tricks to the depths. I will take my revenge on you, my enemy, and I will start with the death of your beloved Judah."

Abel did not reply. Instead, he turned, gazing at that vast army behind Kiran, and called out, "Come to me. It is not yet too late to leave your ways of darkness. Any who will, come. Come now that you may have your life."

The armed hordes stared back at him as if frozen.

My mouth hung open. Why did Abel waste time extending this final mercy? Surely, not a single stone heart among these masses could be stirred, even by such a one as him.

Murmurs, boos, hisses snaked through the crowd. A woman stepped out, her black, matted hair, rows of belted knives, and giant spear giving her a raptor-like appearance. But her hard face shone wet with tears. She threw her weapons and then herself on the ground before Abel. He dismounted, took her hand, and raised her to her feet. Then a man came forward, too, skinny, greasy, trembling. He also was pursued by harsh cries from the crowd. An arrow flew through the air as the man kneeled before Abel, striking the earth by him. He did not turn. Abel took his hand, too, and sent both people behind his front line to safety. "Is there no one else?" he called. The minutes passed. Abel remounted his horse and gazed at Kiran.

"This is your last opportunity, Kiran. Surrender now," Abel commanded.

"Never," Kiran hissed, his eyes ablaze.

Abel gazed at Kiran, his eyes full of sorrow. Then he turned and raised his hand. The massive army lifted their weapons as one. I grabbed my sword and held tight.

We swept over our enemies like a flood.

EPILOGUE

In the summer of the third and final year of the governance of Lady Judah of Castle Marah, the people of the land defeated their enemies.

The battle against Kiran at the southern border did not last long. In the heat of the battle Kiran and a handful of his leaders fled, but no one else on the field of war escaped destruction. The only survivors were two ladies and a lamb. These had been protected by a queenlike, dark-haired woman in shining armor on a golden steed. Her own people had barely recognized her as Judah, and those who did stood in awe of her.

Later, the triumphal procession passed through village upon village of cheering inhabitants, most of whom asked each other who the noble couple was that led such an army and who brought freedom in their wake. The people did not recognize their former governor, nor the man who had lived as the head shepherd among them.

The servants of the Mountain King had been working.

While the mighty army triumphed on the southern kingdom's border, conquering all who embraced rebellion and hated the Mountain King, other servants of the Mountain King labored joyfully to restore Amia to glory. The road to the palace of the Mountain King, which had run through Amia in the days of King Leo and Queen Elanna, had been cleared and ran again through the grounds of the Amia palace. The broken gate and lock had been removed completely. The husbandmen of the Mountain King reestablished the surrounding gardens. They were the same, only *not* the same. Everything thrived in its perfect form, even overshadowing the prior glory. This was true as well of the palace, which was also made new. The once-perfect palace and gardens were somehow even more perfect, true, and lasting than they were before, almost too magnificent for human eye to regard. Upon returning from the battle, Judah and her people had been escorted directly to Amia, as had all the remaining inhabitants of Marah. Abel had greeted every person, and each gratefully swore allegiance to their king.

"Here I leave you until we meet again," Abel told Judah when he brought her to Amia, "but there is one thing you must do before you come to me."

She bowed to the ground, saying that first she had a request.

"Tell me, Princess Judah—what do you wish?"

"Please—I wish to be made well, to be whole. I ask that you heal me of the sickness. I ask that my hearing be restored."

"It is good what you have requested," he replied joyfully. "This was the deed about which I spoke." He raised her up and placed his hand gently on the left side of her head over her ear. "Be healed, my beloved."

At that time, Anna had handed her the slim,

golden box which she had carefully retrieved from Marah. Judah, gladness shining in her eyes, took a gold key from around her neck and unlocked the box. "I choose you as you chose me, for you are my beloved, you are my friend," she said softly to Abel as she put the betrothal document with letters of gold into his hands. Suddenly, she began singing the song that only they two could hear, and she sang it with delight. He kissed her hands softly before riding off, leading his army home. He said he would await her arrival in the palace of the Mountain King the following day.

The day of the marriage celebration between Princess Judah and the son of the Mountain King dawned with a glory unprecedented in the history of rising suns. Amia was alive with preparations for the journey to the wedding feast—not only was the bride to be arrayed in glorious, perfect white, but also every single person who chose to come, both high and low of birth, prepared to attend in their wedding clothes.

Anna and Hilda and Raven all fussed most carefully over the princess, and how right and true the title was. Abel had declared her restored to the title as she joined him at the head of the army when they left Marah for the southern border. He had called for a specific box to be brought from the treasury in Marah. The box revealed a delicate crown of tiny golden leaves that had been given to Judah when she was born, a gift of the Mountain King. Abel set this carefully on Judah's dark head, where it shone with a radiance matched only by Judah's glowing face.

When the time came to depart for the palace of the

Mountain King, the inhabitants of Amia presented in their wedding finery to greet the bride. A great cheer erupted as Princess Judah appeared at her doors, and all the people gathered flowing around and behind her. Truly, never has a more noble procession been seen by the eyes of men than that which accompanied the bride of the son of the Mountain King as she walked to her beloved.

The bride's eyes and face flashed with glory and joy. Her white gown of silk and fine linen was veiled with the long, splendid robe she had received as a gift from the son of the Mountain King. Her star diamond necklace outshone the sun, and the coronet of golden leaves that rested in her rich hair proclaimed her position as princess. Two smiling ladies dressed in magnificent gowns attended her, carefully lifting the bridal train. They were followed by the quiet-faced Raven, whose eyes betrayed gladness, dressed still in white, her black hair cascading over her shoulders and her arms overflowing with fragrant blossoms from the gardens of Amia. Behind, marched the people of the kingdom, all of whom had been invited to the marriage supper of the son of the Mountain King.

Ahead of the marriage procession lay their destination, but who can describe the glories of the palace of the Mountain King? Tales shared that a great feast was spread for thousands of guests. The beauty and joy of the groom and bride were beyond ability to tell. But of the marvelous wedding feast, the magnificence of the palace itself, the trumpet song as the son of the Mountain King and his wife took their places on the thrones—these are beyond rendering. Perhaps, reader of this scroll, one day you will long to know what they have seen.

Perhaps the only way to know is to follow the path of those who have been before, and go yourself, reader, to the halls of the Mountain King. His palace is vast and all are welcome.

There is always room for more.

We love Him because He first loved us.
~ 1 John 4:19

Author's Note

Writing a book is a genesis, a journey, a dream, and it does not happen in isolation. I will always be indebted to those who helped shape these words.

First thanks belong to my family, especially my beloved husband, teammate, and best friend, Greg. Not only have you supported four NaNoWriMo sessions—that's one-hundred-twenty total days of crazy wife writing—but also you have read my roughest drafts and taken care of the kiddos and household so that I could revise, edit, repeat. Your love shines daily of the Great Love. And thank you to my favorite girls, Lois and Dana. You will understand later what I've been working on; this book is for you, sweet daughters.

Next thanks belong to my parents, who first taught me the ultimate love story: the love of God for humanity. You have never stopped showing me this love and guiding me on the solid path. Mom, thank you for weaving storytelling and word-love into the fiber of my being. You have always made me believe I'm a writer and that my words have weight. Dad, thank you for reading us everything from Tolkien to Spurgeon and for training me to use my mind. I've always known you are proud of me, and that gives me wings.

Thank you to my sisters, who are my besties, my co-adventurers, my heroes. Without you three, we wouldn't be a foursome. You are my cheer squad, my book buddies, and the only people with whom I'll ever stalk an elephant in the wilds of northern Mozambique (because I probably shouldn't do that twice). Julia and Kristy, thank you for reading my rough drafts and giving me the best feedback a writer could ask for in purple pen. Your early confidence in this story meant the world to me. Elly, I owe you a greater debt than I can repay for being my first editor, "Els the Eliminator." You forge, you compress, you illuminate, you distill. Thank you for helping me prune the superfluous so the essential could thrive.

So many thanks to my other incredible beta readers for their time, insightful feedback, and encouragement: Theresa Arnold; Carolyn Halvarson and her husband Arne, who is now with the Lord; Papa Rick Forrester; Mom (Sylvia) and Mom (Dawn). Thank you to the wonderful family and friends who comprise my support team with their enthusiasm, kind words, and interest throughout this process: Grace King; Mary Forrester; Aunt Jeannie Mertens; friends in Romania & Mozambique; the Chapter One ladies; Jennifer Hillman-Magnuson, who first encouraged me to pursue publication; Dad (Nathaniel) and Dad (Allen); my bros-in-law, Justin, Tom, & Ethan; my extended family. I also must acknowledge the influence my nieces and nephews have on me daily, bringing so much joy and reminding me of the hope to come: Evi and Leif; Lena and James; Nate and Lydia; Erik and the others who are already playing in Heaven.

Further, I want to acknowledge the special group of people to whom I dedicate this book. My students—you're all grown up now, out changing the world!—

inspired me to persist in growing as a person, writer, and reader. Alongside them, I am grateful to the brilliant, generous coworkers who brought so much joy to my years teaching at Abiqua School and who continue to cheer for me on this journey. I treasure every single one of you.

Finally, my gratitude to my editor, Fay Lamb, is endless. You truly saw this story, and you opened a door. Your astute vision, discernment, and encouragement has made this experience the greatest gift. I have learned from you, leaned on your expertise, and loved every minute of this journey. Thank you also to Nicola and the entire staff team at Pelican Book Group—you have welcomed me and made the path smooth. Thank you for investing your time and talents in this book, for your prayers and patience, for caring about this story.

May these words kindle hearts.

All glory to God.

Thank you…

for purchasing this Harbourlight title. For other inspirational stories, please visit our on-line bookstore at www.pelicanbookgroup.com.

For questions or more information, contact us at customer@pelicanbookgroup.com.

Harbourlight Books
The Beacon in Christian Fiction™
an imprint of Pelican Book Group
www.pelicanbookgroup.com

Connect with Us
www.facebook.com/Pelicanbookgroup
www.twitter.com/pelicanbookgrp

To receive news and specials, subscribe to our bulletin
http://pelink.us/bulletin

May God's glory shine through
this inspirational work of fiction.

AMDG

You Can Help!

At Pelican Book Group it is our mission to entertain readers with fiction that uplifts the Gospel. It is our privilege to spend time with you awhile as you read our stories.

We believe you can help us to bring Christ into the lives of people across the globe. And you don't have to open your wallet or even leave your house!

Here are 3 simple things you can do to help us bring illuminating fiction™ to people everywhere.

1) If you enjoyed this book, write a positive review. Post it at online retailers and websites where readers gather. And share your review with us at reviews@pelicanbookgroup.com (this does give us permission to reprint your review in whole or in part.)

2) If you enjoyed this book, recommend it to a friend in person, at a book club or on social media.

3) If you have suggestions on how we can improve or expand our selection, let us know. We value your opinion. Use the contact form on our web site or e-mail us at customer@pelicanbookgroup.com

God Can Help!

Are you in need? The Almighty can do great things for you. Holy is His Name! He has mercy in every generation. He can lift up the lowly and accomplish all things. Reach out today.

Do not fear: I am with you; do not be anxious: I am your God. I will strengthen you, I will help you, I will uphold you with my victorious right hand.

~Isaiah 41:10 (NAB)

We pray daily, and we especially pray for everyone connected to Pelican Book Group—that includes you! If you have a specific need, we welcome the opportunity to pray for you. Share your needs or praise reports at http://pelink.us/pray4us

Free eBook Offer

We're looking for booklovers like you to partner with us! Join our team of influencers today and periodically receive free eBooks!

For more information
Visit http://pelicanbookgroup.com/booklovers